☠ PYRATES #2

EYE OF ETERNITY

CHRIS ARCHER

SCHOLASTIC INC.
New York Toronto London Auckland Sydney
Mexico City New Delhi Hong Kong Buenos Aires

ISBN 0-439-36852-9

Copyright © 2003 17th Street Productions,
an Alloy, Inc. company
All rights reserved.
Published by Scholastic Inc.

Produced by 17th Street Productions,
an Alloy, Inc. company
151 West 26th Street
New York, NY 10001

12 11 10 9 8 7 6 5 4 3 2   3 4 5 6 7 8/0

Printed in the U.S.A.   40
First Scholastic printing, February 2003

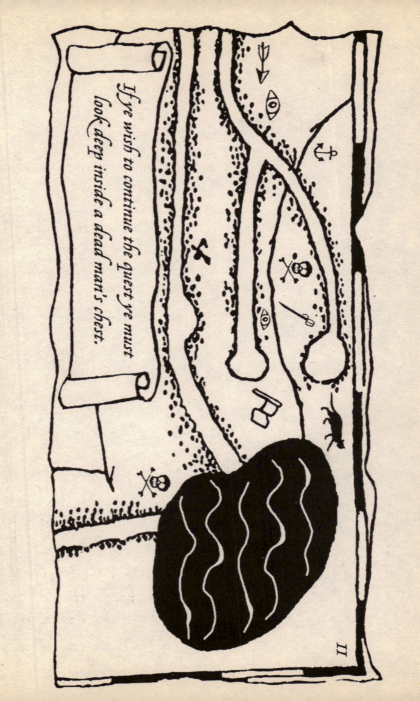

If ye wish to continue the quest ye must look deep inside a dead man's chest.

II

One

Clues

"Hey, look out! You're dripping cheese on it!" George van Gelder reached out with a napkin just in time to catch a gob of gooey mozzarella before it fell on the ancient journal of Captain Kidd. Derrick Wilson, George's best friend, looked sheepishly at the piece of pizza in his hand and yanked it away from the old book. George was too excited about the journal to even think about eating, but that hadn't stopped his friends.

"Oops! Sorry," Derrick said.

"Hey, are you going to eat that?" Shannon Starling asked.

"Yeah. I mean, no." Derrick shook his head and dropped the pizza onto his plate. "I'm kind of stuffed. You want it?"

"Sure, thanks." Shannon reached out for the slice and took a couple of bites. Next to her, Renee Kozinski wrinkled her nose.

"Yuck," she said. "Derrick's mouth touched that pizza. You're getting his germs!"

"Oh, whatever." Shannon took another bite and rolled her eyes. "After that spit sandwich when we all took the pyrate's oath, I think we already have plenty of each other's germs!"

"Gross!" Derrick groaned. "Don't remind me. My hand still feels slimy." He leaned over George's shoulder and scanned the page George was reading. "Anyway, who cares about the pizza? We're all here to check out the journal."

George shifted to make room for Shannon and Renee to see, too. The four of them were crowded around the most precious artifact George had ever seen. It was a journal—a three-hundred-year-old leather-bound book—that had actually belonged to Captain Kidd, the notorious pirate. The journal was valuable in and of itself, but who knew what other treasures it might reveal?

George and his friends had found it buried in a cave, in a tunnel deep beneath his house in downtown Manhattan. It had been a little over a week since they had located the cave by following an old treasure map that was hidden away in the secret compartment of a desk in his attic. George's house had been built by the infamous pirate Captain Kidd, a man whose seafaring adventures had fascinated George for as long as he could remember. He was thrilled at the idea that there might be treasure left by Kidd near his house.

The cave where they had found the journal was part of a complex system of tunnels—a secret underground world. George still got goose bumps when he thought about it. *This can't really be happening to me,* he kept thinking. *Pirates? Treasure? Secret tunnels underneath my house?*

But it was.

And it had changed George's whole life.

Dad would never believe any of it, George thought, flipping a page of the journal. *In fact, he'd freak out!* Peter van Gelder was a history scholar. To him, history was something confined to books, books, and more books—not something that could happen right here, right under his house. George's mom probably would have loved this kind of adventure. She had been a history professor, too, but she had seen the world in a different way. She got excited about things. She had totally been into pirates, and she'd passed her obsession on to George. But she had died when George was five, and since then it had been just him and his father. If George told his dad about what he and his friends had found, his dad would want to verify the map with books, colleagues, maybe even run scientific tests. George and his friends would never see the map again—let alone be able to track down the treasure. Peter van Gelder was a great dad, but he was awfully short on imagination.

So his dad was never *going* to find out, at least not if George could help it. Right now this whole adventure was a huge secret that only the four friends knew about. And George intended to keep it that way.

He glanced at his watch. His dad would be home from his Tuesday night bridge game at nine-thirty. They didn't have much time.

"Listen to this," George said, his voice rising as he skimmed the journal page. He was almost too excited to concentrate. He'd been waiting a whole week to look at the journal, because he'd promised his friends he wouldn't read any of it until the four of them could look at it together. "It says here in Captain Kidd's last will and testament that he buried the 'Eye of Eternity' somewhere in Manhattan—'under this house, to protect the safety of my beloved wife, Sarah.'"

"That's your great-great-great-grandmother, right?" Renee asked.

"Eight greats," George corrected her. Captain Kidd was practically a relative of his—Kidd had married Sarah Oort, George's great-great-great-great-great-great-great-great-grandmother. (Whew!)

Unfortunately, George wasn't *actually* a descendant of Kidd—Sarah Oort had married another man, Ulysses Pyle, after Kidd's hanging. George's family was descended from him.

"That's cool, but what *is* the Eye of Eternity?" Derrick asked, scratching his head through his dark cornrows.

"According to this, it's 'the precious and legendary gem of the Litarian king,'" George read from the journal. "'So beautiful is it, and its power so vast, that its loss has pushed the proud nation of Litaria into chaos. Since its unlawful theft in 1678, the Litarians have known only war and squalor.'" George glanced up at his friends. "Wow. That sounds intense." He turned back to the journal. "'While I am unable to return the diamond, I confess that its rightful place is in the hands of the Litarian monarchy.'"

"A *diamond*?" Derrick gaped at the journal. "Captain Kidd buried a *diamond* under your house? Cool!"

Shannon's eyes widened, and she moved closer to get a better look at the journal. "But what about the other part?" she asked. "The Litarian monarchy—isn't that one of the countries your *dad* studies?"

"Actually, yeah," George explained. "My dad studies eastern European history, and he has written a couple of papers about Litaria. It's really academic stuff."

"Weird," Derrick muttered. He walked over to the freezer and pulled out a carton of chocolate ice cream. "Mind if I sample some of this, George?"

George shook his head. "No problem. Get me a spoon, too."

Derrick grabbed some bowls and spoons and started scooping out ice cream. Then he paused and made a face, like he was trying to figure something out. "And now their diamond just so happens to be buried right under your house?"

"Wait, catch me up!" Renee leaned over to look at the journal herself. Her long blond hair brushed over the yellowed page. "*What* is Litaria? And what does your dad have to do with it?"

George grabbed a spoon and pressed it into the softening ice cream. "Sorry, Renee. I forgot you weren't there when we found the map. Litaria is a tiny little country in Europe. It had one of the longest-running monarchies, but then it became part of the Soviet Union. Now it's an independent country again, but things are pretty messed up. The government is corrupt, and most of the Litarian people are poor. A lot of them want to have the king and queen back in power—to get the government back in shape." George licked the ice cream off his spoon. "It's pretty complicated. If you get my dad started, he'll talk about it for days."

Renee shook her head. "Derrick's right. That really is weird," she said.

"I guess." George shrugged. "My dad's interested in a lot of weird things."

"No, that's not what I meant." Renee's eyes lit up and she sat up straight. She looked like she was on to something. "Don't you think it's kind of odd that your dad is an expert on Litaria—the exact same country mentioned in Captain Kidd's journal? And that there's a huge diamond from that exact same country buried under your house?"

Hmmm. Now that she mentioned it, George had to agree. It *was* pretty weird.

But what did it mean?

Could his dad possibly *know* about the diamond?

"How could he know so much about Litaria and not know that the diamond's buried here?" Renee asked.

"Maybe he's already found the Eye of Eternity?" Derrick guessed, not sounding too happy about it.

"But if he had, you'd be rich," Shannon said, tugging thoughtfully on her red-and-orange-streaked ponytail. "And you're not."

"No," George said, mulling it over. "We're pretty much average."

George and his dad lived in a very nice house on Windsor Lane, an old street in lower Manhattan. It was true that not many people in New York City could afford to have a whole house to themselves. But George's house had been in the family for over three hundred years. Before she died, his mother had inherited it from the descendants of Sarah Oort. Otherwise he and his dad would probably be living in an apartment, like most of his friends.

"There's no way he's found the diamond," George went on, thinking out loud. "For one thing, my dad's never even seen this journal. We just dug it up from that cave last week."

Shannon nodded. Derrick started to look hopeful.

"And for another thing," George said after a minute of pondering, "it says right here that you have to have *four* treasure maps to find the Eye of Eternity. We've only got one map so far. He must know that the diamond exists, but I bet he has no idea where it's buried."

"Okay, I guess you're right," Renee said. "But it's still weird that he's an expert on Litaria."

"Weird, but just a coincidence," George agreed.

Derrick leaned over George to look back at the journal. "So does it say how big this Eye of Eternity was?" He ran his hand over the yellowed page. "I guess if it belonged to a king . . . it's huge!"

"Don't start spending the money so fast," Shannon teased. "We still don't know where it is."

Derrick didn't seem to hear her. "It could be the size of a marble," he guessed. "Or as big as an egg!"

"Calm down, money man." Renee put a hand on his shoulder. "Remember: We're splitting the loot four ways."

"It could be as big as a grapefruit!" Derrick was completely ignoring Renee. His eyes were lit up with diamond fever.

"But we've got to *find* it first," George said. "Which means we have to find the other three maps. So let's start looking for clues to find map two." He started flipping the pages of Captain Kidd's journal. The book was thick and dusty, and the pages were scratchy to the touch. George guessed that the paper had stiffened over the years, but he also could tell that paper in the 1600s wasn't anything like what they used today. The words were hard to read, written in thick black ink in a blotchy, old-fashioned script on faded yellow pages. *Captain Kidd's own script.* George shivered at the thought.

The truth was, most of the pages weren't very interesting. Captain Kidd had used his journal to record everything—even boring business transactions. The journal was filled with strange names, dates, and lists of pirate loot that Captain Kidd and his crew had collected. Or rather, "prizes," as the loot was properly called, since Kidd was a privateer, hired by the king of England to raid other countries' ships. He was like a licensed pirate.

George noted as he skimmed that a few of the pages had some really good stuff—like the part dated October 1697, where it said:

I fear that my days of kinship with the British Crown may come back to haunt me. I no longer know who might be trusted and who might not. I sense that my enemies draw nearer to me. That my old friend William gets closer with every breath. I know not how much longer I have. I would do anything to protect my sweet Sarah, to keep her from heartache.

George felt a tingle of excitement as he read over the page. "My sweet Sarah"! That was his great-times-eight grandmother, Sarah Oort! But George wondered what Captain Kidd meant by "my enemies draw nearer. . . . My old friend William gets closer." Who was William? And why was he so frightening to Captain Kidd, who could hold his own with virtually anybody? George couldn't figure it out. Maybe he was the guy sent to arrest Kidd before he was hanged?

Much of the journal was too hard to read, and George skimmed over the dull parts. What time the sun rose every day. How stormy the seas were. How many fish Kidd's crew caught. How many pounds of flour were left in the galley. Who knew Captain Kidd was such a stickler for detail?

"Finding anything?" Renee asked, peering over George's shoulder.

"Um . . . not much." George kept reading. He had flipped to the last pages of the book. Whoa— this section was totally different! It looked like this was where the important stuff was written. *This* was where Kidd talked about the Eye of Eternity.

"What about these? They look like clues," he said as he swung the book around so his friends could see.

In an old-fashioned script it said:

Map №2: If you seek eternity, you must snatch nine lives from a dead man's hand.

"Cool!" Shannon said. "So we're looking for a *corpse!*"

"Oh, gross!" Derrick heaved a sigh. "As if it's

not creepy enough in those tunnels. Now we're hunting for a dead *body*?"

"Not a body," Renee corrected him. "That book was written three hundred years ago. By now the body is probably just a pile of bones."

Derrick shivered. "Yuck. I think I just lost my appetite."

"Not me." Shannon grinned as she grabbed a bowl and scooped out some ice cream. "I can't wait to get down there again. This is where the adventure really begins! We have three maps to find, and then—treasure city!"

"Eat fast," George said, checking the clock again. "My dad will be home in *exactly* one hour and fifty-five minutes. We've got to get going so we can be back here before he comes home."

Renee laughed as if she thought George was being a little silly. But Derrick shook his head. "No kidding—George is right. His dad is always *exactly* on—"

Just then the front door opened.

"George?" a man's voice called out.

George's heart raced.

Oh, no! he thought. *Dad!*

"What's he doing home *now*?" he whispered to his friends.

Two

Delayed

"Dad?" George swallowed hard, peering out into the hall. He felt frustrated and tense. *We were going to go underground! Now it's too late! There's no way we'll be able to check out these clues tonight!* He stifled a groan.

In the ten seconds it took his dad to reach the kitchen from the front door, Shannon managed to whisk Captain Kidd's journal away and throw a dish towel on top of it. She stuffed it on a low shelf near the fridge. But a corner of the musty old leather was still peeking out.

Don't look at it, George warned himself. *Whatever you do, don't look at the book.* He didn't want his father to follow his gaze and see what they'd been hiding.

"How come you're home so early?" George asked his father as he greeted George with a smile.

"Oh, I just came back to get a copy of last month's *Historical Hours* magazine. James St. John and I were discussing an article in it," Peter van Gelder explained.

He lingered by the kitchen doorway expectantly, as if he were waiting to be included in the conversation. But George and his friends were so surprised, no one moved or spoke.

"So you're not staying? You're going *back* to the St. Johns'?" George finally asked.

The St. Johns were a British couple who lived in the house next door and owned an electronics store in midtown. George's father played bridge with them every Tuesday night. Plus, they were always "popping in for tea" or to have a leisurely chat.

"Back to the St. Johns'? Yes, yes, I am." His father nodded and tugged at the brown tweed vest he was wearing. But he still didn't budge from the doorway. George was beginning to feel like time had slowed down. But at least his dad wasn't home to stay. That would have ruined their plans for sure.

Fidgeting, George tried not to look at the clock. There wasn't much time left. If they were going to go underground, they had to hurry up and get his dad out of there.

"So, what are you kids up to?" his father asked cheerfully.

"Nothing," George started to say. Then he noticed that his father was staring at Shannon's notebook, which was lying on the table.

It was a spiral-bound notebook with black pages.

Shannon was one of the coolest girls in the sixth grade—and she was the *only* girl George knew who had her own band. So of course she wrote on black paper. Mostly she used the notebook to write down song lyrics for her band—but now it was filled with notes from Captain Kidd's journal. Words like *EYE OF ETERNITY*. And *FOUR MAPS!!* Screaming out in pink and silver gel ink.

"Is that *pink* ink?" Mr. van Gelder asked, moving closer. His eyes opened in astonishment.

"Yes," Shannon said. She snatched up the notebook and flipped to a clean page as fast as she could. "Actually, I'm, um . . ." She looked up at George's dad. George realized that he was holding his breath, waiting for Shannon to come up with something. "I'm doing a social studies report for school on the nation of Litaria."

"Litaria?" George's father stood up straighter, almost in surprise. He looked strangely pleased, like George thought *he* must look when somebody wanted to talk about pirates. "How did you happen to pick *that* topic?"

"I, um, actually I drew that country out of a hat." Shannon looked at his dad and smiled. "But I mean, I'm *really* psyched about it. I didn't know much about the Litarians before, but their history is just so *interesting*." Mr. van Gelder looked like he had just won the lottery. George suddenly felt sort of guilty. He'd never taken much of an interest in his dad's work—in fact, George always said that it was "boring." He had never realized he could make his father smile like that just by asking him a question about Litaria.

"My report's due next week," Shannon rushed on, "and I don't have enough information yet. And George was just saying that you're an expert on Litaria. So I thought maybe I could ask you some questions."

Derrick shot George an impressed glance. George had to admit that was pretty smooth. Shannon really knew how to think on her feet.

Peter van Gelder beamed. "Why, yes," he said, giving George a pleased-as-punch smile. "I *do* know a bit about Litaria. How can I help?"

"Well, um, I *really* need to know about Litaria in the 1600s," Shannon said. "I've read something about a big diamond? Do you know anything about that?"

George's dad nodded slowly. "Yes," he said. "I do. There is a scepter, called the wolf's head scepter, that has been a symbol of power in Litaria for hundreds of years. The Litarian people believed that the enormous diamond embedded in the scepter had special powers. It was called the Eye of Eternity. As a result of its powers, whoever had the scepter had the right to rule the kingdom."

George glanced around at his friends. That fit in with what they'd read in the journal—about the diamond being "the precious and legendary gem of the Litarian king." And about the diamond's "rightful place" being "in the hands of the Litarian monarchy."

"So, how big was the diamond, anyway?" Derrick asked.

Shannon shot Derrick a warning glance, but George's father didn't seem bothered.

"Ah, yes, Derrick," Mr. van Gelder said with a smile. "The diamond is the heart of the matter, isn't it—the key to the whole story. You see, legend has it that the diamond was revealed to the first king of Litaria in a dream. According to the story, the king was told that if the diamond ever passed out of royal hands, the kingdom of Litaria would fall. When he woke up, he headed for the mountains, to the place where he'd been in his dream, and lo and behold—there was the Eye of Eternity."

"Wow," whispered Derrick. "I'd like to have a dream like that."

George's father chuckled. "Wouldn't we all. Anyway, this is what the Litarian people believed. But in the late 1600s, there was growing unrest in Litaria. A small band of revolutionaries decided that the monarchy was corrupt and had to be overthrown. These revolutionaries made up a small minority of the whole population. Most Litarians respected, even revered the monarchy. But the revolutionaries made a drastic move. They stole the scepter in hopes of weakening the monarchy. They thought they'd be better at ruling Litaria than the king and queen."

"And?" George felt like he was going to burst. How come his father had never told him this part of the story before? "What happened to it?"

"What happened?" George's father repeated the question slowly. "War, misery, destruction. There were decades of fighting, which turned into centuries of struggle."

George glanced over at Derrick, who nodded slightly. Again it was just like Kidd had said in the journal, "Since its unlawful theft in 1678, the Litarians have known only war and squalor."

"But what about the scepter? And the diamond?" Shannon asked. "I thought the diamond was supposed to give them power. Like the dream said."

"Well, Litaria did finally get the scepter back," Mr. van Gelder said. "But the diamond was missing. It had been stolen somewhere along the way."

Stolen? George and his friends exchanged quick glances. *That's right! And we know who wound up with it—Captain Kidd!*

"How big was it?" Derrick repeated eagerly.

"Well." Mr. van Gelder lifted his hands in the air and furrowed his eyebrows, like he was trying to remember. "It was about . . ." His hands made a sphere the size of a golf ball, then he frowned and increased it to the size of an orange . . . then he frowned again. He sighed. "Never mind, I'll just show you." Mr. van Gelder suddenly turned to leave the kitchen.

George almost choked. He couldn't believe this.

"You *have* it?" Renee blurted.

"Hmmm?" Mr. van Gelder stopped in the doorway and chuckled. "Oh, heavens, no. But I have a picture. Wait here."

He ran up the stairs, and George and his friends turned to each other. Derrick shook his head. *"Phew!"* he cried. "I really thought he had the diamond for a second."

"Me, too," Shannon agreed. "No offense, George, but I'm glad he doesn't. That means it might still be down there."

George nodded. His dad's reaction had thrown him for a loop, too. A moment later Peter van Gelder returned with a big book in his hands. George squinted at it; it was one of the bulky history books his dad kept in his study. George's dad flipped to a page with a faded portrait. It was an old etching—a black-and-white drawing of a sickly young man with a sad, frightened expression on his face. George wondered just what had gone on in Litaria to make this young man look so scared.

In his hand the man held an ornate scepter with a head in the shape of a snarling wolf.

"Where's the diamond?" Derrick asked, squinting.

"It's not there," Mr. van Gelder said. "It had already been stolen when this portrait was made. But the diamond originally filled the wolf's mouth."

Whoa. George tried to imagine how big that would be. It was hard to tell from the etching.

Derrick was too excited to keep the question inside. "So, how *big* was it? His mouth isn't open very wide," he said. "It looks like the diamond might only be about as big as a dime."

Mr. van Gelder shrugged. "It *is* hard to tell from this drawing," he agreed. "Litarian historians differ on the size. Some say it was as big as a baseball, some say it was as small as a pea. It's been centuries since anyone in Litaria has seen the diamond, and unfortunately, they didn't keep very accurate records in the 1600s."

"So, about how much do you think it would be worth?" Derrick was trying to sound like he was just barely curious, but George knew better.

"Well, because of its history, of course, the diamond is priceless," Mr. van Gelder answered. "The Litarians would give anything to get it back. And the current government of Litaria just might give anything to keep it away from the country's people. But I suppose if someone just happened to find it and sold it on the open market . . ."

George wondered if his dad could sense all of his friends holding their breath.

"I suppose it would bring in at least a million dollars," his father finally decided.

Derrick tried to act casual. But George could see a tiny smile creeping in at the corners of his mouth. Renee sat up straight and looked at George. Her dark eyes widened, and she mouthed the word *wow*.

As for George, his heart sort of skipped a beat.

A million dollars? Buried right beneath his house? This was better than anything he could have imagined.

Only Shannon managed to play it calm and cool. *But then,* George thought, *she's always cool about everything.*

"So," Mr. van Gelder said, closing the book. "Any other questions about Litaria? I could tell you all about the War of the Weakest. That was an interesting period, from 1788 to the mid-1800s."

George glanced at his watch. It was already eight—now they had only an hour and a half to check out the clues in the tunnels! "Um—Dad? Are the St. Johns still waiting for you to finish your bridge game?"

Peter van Gelder looked surprised and quickly checked his watch. "Yes, I guess I should be getting back." He sighed. "Although we aren't playing bridge tonight. Eleanor had to take care of something at the shop. James mentioned some legal problem they're having. Apparently it's taking up a lot of their time."

"Oh, okay." George started backing away from the table. Maybe if they all acted like they were finished here, his dad would take the hint and head out.

"Well, anyway." Finally, his father turned and headed toward the door. "I'll be back at nine-thirty," he promised. "And I'm right next door if you need me."

"Great, Dad," George said, hoping his impatience wasn't too obvious.

"Thanks for your help, Dr. van Gelder," Shannon said.

"Oh, no problem, Shannon," he replied with a smile. "It was my pleasure."

At last the front door closed behind his father.

"All right, guys, come on. We don't have much time." George jumped up from the table.

"Wait, George," Shannon said. She grabbed the journal off the low kitchen shelf. "Just a minute."

"What are you *doing*?" George was really getting impatient now.

"I just have to check something in the journal again," Shannon said.

"Why?" Renee asked. She bounced nervously, looking at the clock. "We've really got to hurry, Shannon. My mom's going to pick me up at nine-thirty."

"I know." Shannon nodded. "But right before George's dad came in, I saw something on one of the journal pages. I think I know where the diamond is!"

Three

DARK DANGERS

"WHERE?"

George, Derrick, and Renee all shouted it at once.

Shannon just opened the journal quietly, without answering. Carefully, she turned the pages until she found the one she was looking for.

"Here." She pointed triumphantly to a short passage. "See?"

All four of them leaned over to read the page.

In Kidd's thick black script it said:

Find the flag I sail under, and you'll find your eternal reward.

"Get it?" Shannon asked. "Eternal! As in the Eye of *Eternity*!"

"I don't get it, though." Renee cocked her head. "What about the maps? And where's this flag he's talking about, anyway?"

Shannon looked to George expectantly, like he

was supposed to explain the whole thing, but he just frowned. "Ummm . . ."

Shannon sighed in frustration. "Remember you were telling us how you talked to Paul and showed him the map?"

George nodded. He hoped she wasn't *mad* that he'd shown the map to Paul, the homeless boy they'd met who lived in the tunnels. Paul had lived in the tunnels all his life—it was the only world he knew. Paul had gotten George out of one major jam, and he'd thought maybe Paul could help them figure out the map, too.

"You said he pointed to the skull and cross-bones on the map," Shannon said.

"Sure," George replied. "The Jolly Roger."

"He said he'd seen a bunch of stuff with that symbol in a room in the tunnels. Well, I'll bet one of those things is the flag. A flag with the Jolly Roger—'the flag I sail under'!"

George looked at the ceiling and thought. He had to hand it to Shannon—she was sharp. But something about this clue gave him a funny feeling in the pit of his stomach. Something wasn't quite right. If Kidd said they needed all four maps to find the treasure, why would he put in a shortcut? George didn't like shortcuts. He liked to do a job the normal way and get it right. But he could see that everyone else was really excited.

"What's a Jolly Roger again?" Renee asked, looking puzzled.

"A pirate flag. Black, with a white skull and crossbones," George explained. "Um, the only thing is, Kidd *wasn't* a pirate. He was a privateer. There's a big difference. He was licensed to do what he did—he wasn't just a thief."

"Oh, who *cares*?" Shannon said. She was too excited to nitpick. "Maybe he used the Jolly Roger when he got mad at the king and decided to keep some of the loot for himself. I don't know. The point is, there's a flag down there, underground, and the diamond might be there! So we've got to find it!"

George's stomach still felt all funny. He wondered if he should say something else. But then he considered the possibility that Shannon was right—and he shivered with excitement. *If she's right, we could have the diamond in our hands by the end of tonight! We could all be rich!*

"Well, what are we waiting for?" Derrick asked. "Let's do it!" He had gotten up from the table and was already halfway to George's basement. George, Shannon, and Renee looked at each other.

"Well?" asked Renee.

George looked at his two good friends. "The thing is . . . shortcuts don't always work."

Renee seemed to consider this answer. Shannon looked like she was listening, too, but she also looked kind of impatient.

"But what if it *does* work, George?" she asked. "We can go down there and check it out. We won't take any chances. And if I'm right and we can find this room, we might get the diamond tonight!" She looked at him eagerly.

"Well . . ." George thought about Shannon's words. She was right. . . . There was no harm in trying. As long as they were cautious. "Okay," he said finally. "We'll find Paul and try to find the room. But we have to be *careful*."

"All *right*!" Renee grinned. "Come on, George, we'd better get down there. Derrick's probably all rigged up already!" They jumped up and practically tripped over each other following Derrick downstairs.

By now the four of them were experts at getting underground. It only took them ten minutes to put on the climbing gear—harnesses, ropes, helmets, and gloves—that Renee had borrowed from her mountain-climbing and cave-exploring parents. Since she was the climbing expert, it was her job to make sure everyone was hooked up right. She made some quick but thorough examinations and proclaimed everybody good to go.

After that, getting to the secret door that led down to the tunnels was a team effort. First they had to move the boxes that covered a hole in the basement wall. Then one by one they ducked into the open space below George's chimney. The room was tiny, dark, and square. Buried in the dirt floor was a wooden trapdoor with an octagonal handle. George grabbed it and opened the door to the secret world. The damp, cool air of the underground tunnels rose up to meet him, and he actually felt excited to get back down there.

One by one they rigged themselves up and slid down the forty-foot rope. The first time George had done this, it had felt like a total nightmare. Cold, rocky, and wet. Sewer rats running around everywhere.

But now it almost felt like returning home.

Most of the tunnels below the streets of New York—the tunnels that had existed back in Captain Kidd's day—had been carved out by natural streams. But now those tunnels had been joined by old abandoned subway tunnels and storage areas. Homeless people lived down there. And a gang of thugs appeared to be in charge. On an earlier trip, George and his friends had seen those guys threatening Paul. They weren't kidding, either. Paul had gotten away, but George would do anything to avoid another run-in with the thugs.

A few minutes later all four of them were on the ground, standing in a few inches of water that remained in the old underground stream. George could feel the water seeping into his sneakers and making his feet feel squishy. At the base of their entrance was an old log. George had seen it before, but suddenly it struck him as odd. Where had it come from? It wasn't like there were trees growing in these underground tunnels.

"Hey, guys," he said. "Do you ever wonder what this is?"

"No," said Shannon flatly. "Come on, George, we don't have much time. The diamond awaits."

"It just seems weird." George walked over and ran his hand over the ancient wood. It was completely smooth. He wondered how long it had been down there.

"It's trash," said Derrick. "There's nothing weird about that. There's plenty of trash and building junk in the tunnels, from the subway."

But George didn't answer him. He was feeling a spot near the underside of the log. It felt like there was a little carving there—letters, maybe?

He flicked on his light.

"George, it's already eight-twenty," Renee urged gently.

"'Campbell's Yard,'" George read from the wood. "'Boston, Massachusetts. 1683.'" He stood up and faced his friends. "What do you think that means?"

Now Renee looked interested. She walked over and flicked on her own helmet light to study the carving. "That *is* weird," she said. "What would be labeled like that?"

"Guys, come on," Shannon coaxed. "We'll talk about it on the way. We're looking for the *diamond,* remember?"

"The diamond," echoed Derrick. "Come on, guys, no time to waste."

Reluctantly, Renee and George stood up and walked over to their friends.

"Now what?" Renee asked.

Derrick pulled out the treasure map they'd found in the secret compartment of George's dad's desk, up in the attic. Actually it was only a *copy* of the original map, which they'd accidentally locked back in the desk. Derrick had drawn it from his memory, which was practically photographic.

"I guess we find Paul," George said.

"And he leads us to the diamond!" Shannon declared confidently. She started walking down the tunnel.

"You're forgetting two things," Derrick said as they followed the path they'd taken before. It led down the streambed, up a rock pile, and into an abandoned subway station. They had to be extra careful along the way because Captain Kidd had hidden booby traps all along the tunnels. One false move and they could be on the wrong side of a falling boulder. Or a whole tumble of rocks. Or worse!

"What am I forgetting?" Shannon asked. She ducked to avoid hitting her head on a sharp rock.

"One: what it says in the journal," Derrick reminded her. "That we need all *four* maps to find the Eye of Eternity."

"That's not what it said," Shannon argued. "It said something about—"

"Actually, I can tell you *exactly* what it said," Derrick interrupted.

"Oh, of course. I forgot that you're Mr. Photographic Memory." George noticed that Shannon's voice revealed a hint of jealousy. George couldn't blame her. He'd like to be able to memorize everything he saw, too. Though he was a little annoyed that Derrick was bringing this up *now,* when he'd been the first to jump at the shortcut idea. "So, what did it say *exactly*?" she asked.

"It said: 'Beware! One map leads to danger and death. Only he who holds all four maps in his hand will see the true path to eternity,'" Derrick recited.

"So there are definitely four maps," George said,

thinking out loud. "And we need all four maps."

"Maybe not," Shannon argued. "Maybe it just means that *one* of the maps is a fake—a bad one. Maybe if you follow the bad map, it will lead to trouble."

"But what if *that's* the map we have now?" George argued back.

Shannon was quiet for a moment.

"There's something else, too," Derrick said. "What if Paul doesn't want to be found? He wasn't exactly rolling out the red carpet the last time we saw him. He told us to stay out of the tunnels. What if he doesn't *want* to help us?"

Shannon sighed. "I guess we just have to hope he will. I mean, he doesn't hate us or anything. . . . I think he's just not used to having people around."

George had to agree with Derrick. Paul had gotten him out of danger once, but he'd also insisted that George and his friends didn't belong in the tunnels, that they made the place more dangerous. What if he wouldn't help them?

They had come to a tricky spot in the path, a small opening at the top of a rock pile. It led into the abandoned subway station. Only one person at a time could squeeze through.

"I'll go first," George said softly.

No one argued. They had all decided over a

week ago that he was the leader—when they had taken the pyrate oath.

George flipped off the light on his helmet and carefully squeezed through the opening. The last time they had reached this spot, the place had been brightly lit by big electric lights and crawling with thugs who worked for someone named Leroy. There was no doubt this Leroy guy was bad news. But tonight it was quiet. Dark. Empty.

Or *was* it?

In the distance George heard footsteps. *Paul?* George wanted to call out, but he didn't dare. What if it was one of Leroy's henchmen?

He listened again, harder. Another footstep. Or two. They sounded light—not like a two-hundred-pound thug. That made George feel a little more confident.

"Paul?" George called softly.

But there was no answer.

Finally, George flipped on the powerful light attached to his miner's helmet. The beam shot straight through the old cavernous subway station and bounced off the tiled walls on either side.

"Can we come up?" a voice whispered from the hole below him.

George started to say yes, but just then he saw something move in the distance.

It was dark, but George thought it looked like a woman.

He swung his head toward the movement, flashing the light on his helmet in that direction. A long way down the tunnel he could see something move—fast. For half a second George could have sworn that it was a woman with long dark hair, dressed in something close-fitting and black.

George frowned, not sure whether to be frightened or suspicious. Who was she? An underdweller? Someone working for Leroy?

But just as quickly as the figure had come, it darted out of sight.

George blinked and shook his head to clear it. He hadn't really been able to make anything out. Had he imagined the whole thing?

"Um, yeah," he whispered down into the hole where his friends were waiting. "Come on up."

When they had all climbed into the subway tunnel, Renee shone her light through the huge empty space. They were standing where the subway tracks had been, below the platform where commuters would have waited to board the train. The subway station was run-down and sort of spooky, with cracked tiles falling from the walls and rats running rampant on the platform. PROPERTY OF MTA had been stenciled onto one of the metal beams that braced the tunnel.

The MTA was the Metropolitan Transportation Authority—the office that ran the subways.

"It looks so different with the lights gone," Renee said.

"I know," George agreed. "Leroy's men were working here just a week ago. They had lights and all that electronic stuff. You know . . ." Suddenly something clicked in his mind, and he felt his stomach drop in disappointment. "I'll bet they're searching for the treasure, too."

Derrick frowned. "You think?"

"Sure." George looked around the tunnel. "Why else would you come down to these tunnels, bully people around, and have all that equipment? What else could they be looking for? But now they're gone. I wonder why?"

"Maybe they found it," Derrick suggested.

"I don't know," George said. That was his worst fear for sure. "But I'll bet Paul could tell us."

"How are we going to find him, though?" Renee wondered. "We don't really know where he lives. And we don't have a lot of time."

Good question, George thought. They'd been in such a hurry to get into the tunnels, they hadn't really thought this plan through. He checked his watch.

Wow! Forty minutes gone already. George couldn't believe it. "Time flies when you're searching for a million dollars, doesn't it?" he said.

"Maybe we should head down the tracks,"
Renee said, nodding toward a part of the subway
line they had never explored. "At least that way
we might find something new."

It made sense to George. He had already followed
the tracks the other way. The tracks heading . . .

. . . which way?

He looked at his watch again—the new one he'd
just gotten for his birthday. It had a compass on it.
His neighbor, Mr. Roulain, had given it to him.

According to the compass, the other day they'd
gone north. So why not go south now?

Shannon wasn't waiting for him to take the lead
this time. She was already walking along the old
tracks.

George, Renee, and Derrick fell in behind her.

"Is this on the map?" Renee asked.

"No," Derrick said, and George could hear in
his voice that he was pretty nervous about exploring unknown territory.

I am, too, George thought. But the idea of finding the diamond tonight was a pretty powerful
pull. It kept them moving forward.

George pulled the map out of his pocket. "We're
here," he said, pointing to the spot beneath the X
where they'd estimated the subway station would

be. The subway was built long after Captain Kidd's time, so of course it wasn't on the treasure map. "The tunnel on the map extends this way. We'd be about here."

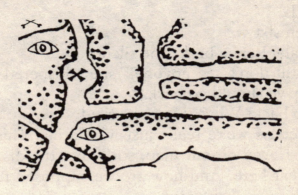

"I'm not sure this was the best idea after all," Renee said. "We're just wandering—"

"Shhh!" George shushed her. He stopped walking and listened.

Were those footsteps again? Behind them?

"Wait," he called to his friends in a whisper. "Hold on a sec."

He listened harder, turning around to shine his light behind them, back toward the subway platform.

Nothing. At least, he couldn't *see* anyone.

But he had this weird chill in his spine that told him someone was back there. Following them.

He listened harder.

"What's wrong?" Derrick whispered.

"I don't know," George answered. "I thought I heard someone."

Everyone stood stock-still for another thirty seconds.

Then sixty.

Finally Renee broke the silence.

"I still don't see anyone," she whispered. "But maybe we should go back."

"Go back? Why?" Derrick asked.

"Because we're really just wandering. This tunnel isn't even on our map, so I'll bet the diamond isn't near here. And how are we supposed to find Paul this way?" she said.

"Well, how do you think we should find Paul?" George asked.

Her silence was an answer of sorts. Unfortunately, none of them had a better plan.

What else could they do except hunt for Paul, try to find the Jolly Roger, follow the clues in the journal, and hope they stumbled onto the remaining three maps?

"Hey! I found something!" Shannon called from farther down the tracks.

She had turned out her light while they were listening for the footsteps. George hadn't realized that she had continued moving forward without them.

"Come look," she called softly.

The three of them hurried down the tracks. Shannon was shining her helmet light at something scrawled on an old metal door in the side tunnel wall. The door was only about four feet high. It seemed to be rusted shut. From the look of it, George figured it must have once been a storage closet for subway switches or equipment or something.

On the door, in white graffiti script, it said:

FOR LEROY'S EYES ONLY!
NO TRESPASSING!

"Wow," Renee said. "What do you think's back there?"

"Don't touch it," Derrick said, quickly backing away. "We don't know who this Leroy guy is."

"It must be something good, though," Shannon said. "I mean, why else would he hide it from everybody else?"

Derrick frowned. "I dunno, I can't explain it. I just have a really bad feeling about this. I say we *don't* open the door."

"Well, it looks like we *can't* open the door," Shannon said, gently feeling its edges. "There's no door handle—no way to pull it open. And look!"

She pointed to the right side of the door—a shiny new lock with a tiny keyhole!

"Whoa," Renee murmured. "It's an old door, but it's definitely gotten some attention recently. That lock looks brand-new."

Shannon pushed at the door, then tried to pry the sides open. "And unfortunately, it's locked."

"Are you sure?" George bent down, shining his light at the bottom edge. There seemed to be a gap underneath, where the cement wall of the subway tunnel had worn away. "Maybe if we can get a hold from underneath . . ." He reached his hand down and stuck his fingers into the gap. Grasping the bottom edge of the door, he pulled hard.

"Still stuck, right?" Shannon asked.

"Yeah." George nodded. "But I think I can get my hand inside. If I can just fit enough fingers in to get a grip, maybe I can pull it. . . ."

He was on his knees now. He stuck his arm into the gap, up under the metal door. He felt around a bit. Dirt, rocks, dirt—*wait* a minute. There was something small, smooth, and cold—it felt like metal.

"Hmmm," said George. "Something's back there. It feels like maybe a Walkman. . . ."

He tried to arrange his fingers around the object so that he could pull it under the door. Finally he was sure he had it between his thumb and forefinger. Very slowly he pulled it closer. . . .

"What is it?" Shannon cried as he eased one side under the door.

"It's . . . it's . . ." Derrick flashed his helmet light on it, squinting to make out the object. "It's a *handheld computer!*"

"A what?" asked Renee. George looked at the tiny computer. It was no bigger than the size of his hand, shiny silver, with a smooth, light-up face. Actually it looked brand-new—not like it had been sitting unnoticed in this tunnel for long. Gently George eased his hand back under the door to see if he could feel anything else.

"A handheld computer," Derrick was saying. "My dad has one. It's like a little Rolodex, calendar, and notebook all in one. You can play games on them. . . . You can even send and receive e-mail. Hey, if this belongs to Leroy, it could have secret info stored on it."

"Cool!" Shannon picked up the computer and looked it over. "Where's the on button?"

George jumped. All at once he felt something else behind the door.

Something moving. Something *alive*.

Something *crawling up his arm!*

George opened his mouth to scream.

Four

Alive

George jerked his arm away so fast, he bumped it on the rusty bottom edge of the door and scraped the skin.

"Owww!" he cried. But he was so freaked out by whatever had climbed up his arm, he barely felt the scrape.

"What's wrong?" Renee shouted, stumbling back to get out of his way.

"Something's *on* me!" George cried. He scampered backward and shook his arm hard, trying to shake off whatever it was.

The light from his helmet lit up the creatures.

Spiders!

Dozens of fat, bulbous white spiders were crawling all over him!

Renee let out a shrill scream, then jumped back and ran in terror toward the subway station.

George shook his arm and brushed at the spiders furiously, knocking them to the ground. His heart was hammering. *Get off me!* he wanted to scream. But he didn't want to look scared in front of his friends. He was the captain, the leader, and it was his job to stay strong.

But he was seriously disturbed by what was happening on his arm. The spiders had some kind of crazy sticking power, like glue. Even when he batted at them, a few of them wouldn't let go. They crawled up higher, toward his underarm.

"Oh, yuck! Yuck! They're *in* my shirt!" George yelled, brushing harder and backing away.

"We have to smash them!" Shannon shouted. "Just squash them or something!"

Gross! George felt queasy at the thought of squashing those fat white bodies on his skin. Especially under his clothes. What would their insides look like? Were they poisonous? He wiggled and shook his shirt, swatting and shaking. Finally, he brushed wildly at what he hoped was the last one. Were there more? Was it possible that it was over?

He felt like they were still on him. Crawling all over him. He felt something under his arm, a sting on the back of his neck.

"Shine your light on me," he yelled at Derrick. "Are they gone?"

The light from Derrick's helmet was so super-bright in George's eyes, he regretted the request almost immediately. He squinted, turning his head away while Derrick checked him out.

"I don't see anything," Derrick said after a minute. "You're clean."

Ick. George shivered. He didn't *feel* clean.

"Let's get out of here," George said. "We don't have much time before my dad gets home. Besides, we kind of lost track of our mission."

"Yeah," Shannon agreed. "Our whole plan was just to find Paul and look around. Next time I guess we should have a better strategy." She looked down at the handheld computer, which was still in her left hand. "At least we found this," she said. "It could really help us figure out what Leroy's up to."

"What happened to Renee?" Derrick asked as they trudged back to the subway platform. "Did she take off? She really looked scared."

"She might have run all the way back to George's house," Shannon said. "She hates spiders. It's her one big phobia."

"I thought she was all about nature," Derrick said. "How can someone who hikes and rock climbs and goes into caves be afraid of spiders?"

Shannon shrugged. "People don't always make sense."

When they squeezed back through the narrow

opening onto the rock pile, Renee was waiting for them in the tunnel. She had her arms wrapped around herself, and she was shivering.

"I'm sorry, guys," she said sheepishly. "I sort of freaked out."

George shrugged. "That's okay. Now we're even."

Renee smiled and shook her head. "No, *I* just have a thing about spiders. *You're* scared of everything from rope climbing to rats! That doesn't make us even!" She laughed.

"Okay, maybe not," George admitted, laughing, too. "Let's just get out of here. My dad will be home soon."

"All right," said Shannon. "But we're coming back tomorrow with a better plan to hunt for Paul and the flag and the diamond. Agreed?"

Renee frowned. "I can't tomorrow," she said. "I've got gymnastics."

Derrick couldn't come over on Thursday night because he had to baby-sit his little brother. And Friday night was a big-deal slumber party for all the girls in their class. So they weren't going to be able to go underground again until Saturday.

George sighed. Saturday seemed an awfully long way off.

"What if Leroy's men *are* digging for the treasure and they find the diamond by then?" George worried.

His friends were silent. He was sure the idea had occurred to them, too. But there were lots of "what ifs." What if they couldn't find Paul? What if the map they were using was the bad one? What if the diamond was long gone—dug up years ago when the buildings and subway tunnels of New York were first built?

"At least we have this computer now," Derrick said after a moment. "Let me take it home. I'm pretty good at this kind of thing. I can try to read some of the files and get an idea of what Leroy's up to."

"All right," George agreed. "Good idea. I guess everything else will have to wait until Saturday." The waiting was going to *kill* George. But he had no choice. It was part of their pyrate oath. He and his friends had agreed that they'd only go underground as a team. Together.

By the time they returned to George's basement, his digital watch said 9:25. There was barely time for Renee to clean up before her mom arrived.

"You know, George," Renee said as they walked up the stairs from the basement, "maybe we should all be doing more to learn about the tunnels when we're not down there. Like, what if I borrowed your *New York Underground* book until we get together again?"

George considered. It wasn't a bad idea. He'd

been so distracted by the pirate history books, he hadn't done much more than leaf through the other book's pages.

"Sure," he agreed after a moment. "Learn all you can. Then maybe you can help us when we come across something in the tunnels that we can't understand."

Renee nodded. She and Shannon ducked into the downstairs bathroom. George and Derrick dragged themselves into the kitchen.

That's when he saw the carton of chocolate ice cream on the kitchen table. Most of it had melted, and the bottom of the carton was leaking.

"Oh, man! We forgot to put the ice cream away!" he moaned, staring at the dark brown puddle spreading on the white tablecloth.

"Wow. Look at it." Derrick leaned over the carton like a scientist. "It's not really liquid. It's still sort of holding together like a milk shake. Only in a totally melted state."

So what? George thought. This was no time for a scientific exploration! His dad was going to be home any minute now!

"I'm going to be in a state of *major trouble* if we don't get this cleaned up," George said.

Frantically, he whisked the carton of ice cream into the sink, grabbed a sponge, and started blotting.

Was it even possible to get a chocolate stain out of white cloth? It didn't look like it.

He checked the clock again. 9:28 P.M. His dad was never late. He'd be here in two minutes. Peter van Gelder was like a human version of one of those atomic clocks. It was like he got the time beamed to him from a satellite.

The front doorbell rang. George held his breath. But it was only Renee's mother.

"Renee, the book is right on my nightstand in my room," he called to her. "You can go get it. I've got kind of a situation here."

He listened to Renee's footsteps as she ran up the stairs and into his room, then back down again.

"Got it! You want a ride?" Renee called to Derrick. "My mom has the car, and she can drop everyone off."

Derrick looked up from the ice cream to shoot George a questioning glance.

"Yeah, it's okay," George said with a nod. "Go. I'll deal with this."

"Thanks. See you tomorrow," Derrick called on his way out the front door.

Exactly two minutes later the front door opened again. Once again, Peter van Gelder was home on the dot. He was like a force of nature.

"George?" he called.

"In here," George answered weakly.

No sense trying to hide the meltdown. His dad was going to see it eventually.

George braced himself for his dad's reaction.

"Hi—" his dad started to say, but his voice died away. He stared at the table, then at the melted ice cream in the sink. "Oh, for heaven's sake, George. What a mess."

"I-I'm sorry, Dad," George stammered. "I tried to clean it up, but . . ."

"Well, chocolate doesn't just jump out of a white tablecloth." George's father walked over to the table and carefully lifted the wet cloth. "This was your mother's favorite tablecloth," he said with a slight frown. "Did you know that?"

"No," George said. Now he felt *terrible*. His dad barely ever mentioned George's mom. Why did she have to come up in reference to something he'd ruined?

"Never mind trying to blot it," his father said. "It'll have to be washed."

"I'm really sorry," George said.

His father shook his head. "I know, George. Just be more careful in the future." Mr. van Gelder turned around and began to gather the tablecloth. He seemed to think that George had left the room. George could see a sort of sadness in his dad's eyes, and he knew it had to do with his mother. George knew he still missed her.

"What else did Mom like?" George blurted out before he'd thought it through.

Mr. van Gelder turned around in surprise. He looked like he'd been caught off guard, like George had just asked him the square root of eight million or something. After a moment the surprise left his eyes and he looked at George curiously.

"Well," he said, as though he wasn't sure how to continue. "She liked a lot of things, George. What do you mean?"

George shrugged. "I don't know." He reached into his pocket and felt the tiny gold locket his mother had given him, with what he'd believed until recently was her own picture carved inside in ivory. When George and his friends had found the pirate map, he'd realized that it was actually a picture of his great-times-eight grandmother, Sarah Oort, who'd looked amazingly like his mother. Even though George's memories of his mother were faint, he still missed her sometimes. He carried the locket all the time because it reminded him of her.

"George?"

George shook off his thoughts and looked at his father, who was giving him a quizzical stare, like he'd been trying to get his attention for a while.

"Yeah, Dad?"

"I said, it's getting late. I think you should get ready for bed."

George's dad had the bunched-up tablecloth in his hands, and now he walked toward the doorway and flicked off the light. "I think I'll stay down here and read for a while," he said.

"Good night, Dad." George turned and began to climb the stairs. "I'm really sorry about the tablecloth."

His father nodded slightly. "I know, George. Good night."

In his room George put on his pajamas and lay awake for a while before he could fall asleep. He had a lot to think about: his dad, his mom, and the tunnels. He chose to focus on the last one. How would he and his friends find Paul again? And could the clue Shannon had found really lead them to the diamond?

Well, George thought with a sigh, *I guess it'll be Saturday before any of us find out.*

Five

SNEAKING

George looked out the window in his room, feeling like he might burst with anticipation.

After one of the longest weeks he could ever remember, it was *finally* Saturday. He'd talked to his friends at school every day, but there wasn't much new to report—Derrick said that the computer they'd found had some kind of security program that wouldn't let you in without a password. He'd been madly trying to come up with every code he thought Leroy might use, but he didn't really know much about him, and it was taking forever.

Now George scanned the people below on Windsor Lane, hoping to pick Derrick out of the crowd.

Windsor Lane was near the heart of New York's financial district—close to Wall Street. During the week the area was pretty crazy. But on a Saturday his street got fairly quiet. It was lined with some of the oldest houses in New York. The people on the sidewalks were mostly just his neighbors. People like Mr. Roulain, who lived down the street.

In fact, there Mr. Roulain was right now! He was standing on the corner, talking to somebody. When George leaned forward, he could see that Mr. Roulain was finishing up a conversation with the St. Johns. He watched him say good-bye, then stroll off down the street. He had a leather backpack slung over his shoulder, bursting with groceries. George smiled. *Mr. Roulain is a cool guy,* he thought. He always had a laid-back attitude. He dressed pretty cool, too. Jeans. Sweater. Leather boots.

Not like Peter van Gelder, who wore old man clothes, like tweed vests and suspenders.

"George?" His dad knocked on his door. George was watching the street so intently, he jumped.

"Hey, Dad," he called.

"May I come in?" his father asked.

George sighed. Not that he minded talking to his father, but Derrick was going to be there any minute.

"Sure," he said reluctantly.

Mr. van Gelder opened the door and stepped into George's room with a hesitant smile. As he entered, George could see that he was holding an old letter in his hands. "I thought you might want to see this," his father said.

"What is it?" George asked.

"Well, this is the first letter I ever got from your mother," his father answered. "When we were in college. I just came across it in my desk. I remembered you were asking about her Tuesday night and thought you might be interested."

George nodded quickly, swinging his legs over the side of his bed. "From Mom? Yeah, let me see."

His father handed the letter to him slowly. Carefully. As if he were afraid to damage it. George opened the pale blue envelope and pulled out the single sheet. The writing was in dark blue ink, with an old-fashioned fountain pen. That seemed right somehow for George's parents—a couple of old-fashioned historians. George read the letter; it was short.

Dear Peter,
   Isn't it romantic that we both love the same things? March instead of April. Vanilla more than chocolate. Rain much more than snow.
   And history, with all its incredible stories. I feel so lucky to have met you. Let's talk again soon.
                          Marianne

Wow, George thought, holding the letter tightly. There was something about reading this old letter that made him feel closer to his mother than he ever had before.

"I don't remember much about her," George admitted to his dad.

"Oh, that's not surprising," his father said in a kind voice. "You were so young when she died."

"I remember that she liked the color blue," George said. "And she used to try to make up stories for me based on her history books. And she liked to play old jazz records."

George looked at his father. He was smiling wistfully. "That's all true," he said.

"Where are her records now?" George asked.

"They're in a box in the basement," his dad said. "Maybe we could play them sometime."

George wondered whether that was one of the boxes blocking the entrance to the trapdoor. He frowned and turned back to the letter.

"I like vanilla more than chocolate, too," he said.

"I know you do," his father said with a smile. "That's why I thought you'd like to see this letter."

"Do you think it's genetic?" George asked.

His father laughed. "Could be."

"But I'm not with you guys on the rain part." George shook his head.

"I know that, too," Peter van Gelder said, still smiling.

This is great, George thought. Having his dad bring this letter in. But it was strange, too. His dad didn't talk much about his mom. It seemed like he missed her too much. After George's mom had died, his dad had taken down all of her pictures. It was like he couldn't bear to look at her face anymore.

"Do you have other letters I could see?" George asked.

His father was quiet.

"Ummm, I'll think about it." He paused again.

"Was she really a lot like you?" George asked. "I mean, did she love history just as much?"

His father nodded slowly. "She did," he said. "In fact, she's the one who got me interested in Litaria."

"Really?" George wanted to hear more. "How?"

"Well, it was when we were in college," his father said carefully. His eyes stared off, as if he was trying to remember. "She read the story about the Litarian scepter and the diamond, and she thought it was intriguing somehow. Romantic, I guess."

I wonder if she knew Captain Kidd had the diamond, George thought. But no. There was no way. How could she? She hadn't seen the journal.

Except . . . neither had Leroy's men. The thugs underground. *They* hadn't seen the journal, but *they* seemed to know about Captain Kidd's treasure. How did *they* find out?

George's father was staring at him. George guessed he had been quiet for a long time.

"So you started studying up on Litaria after that?" George asked.

"Yes," his father said. "And we—"

But then the front door buzzer rang, interrupting their conversation.

"Who could that be?" George's father asked, glancing out the window.

George jumped up. "Oh, it's probably Derrick," he said. "He's coming over." He looked at his dad, feeling torn: On the one hand, he loved hearing stories about his mom. But on the other hand, there were the tunnels and the diamond. . . .

"I'd better get that." George hurried out of his room, past his dad. He took the steps fast, almost too fast, and yanked open the front door.

"Hi," Derrick said. "You by yourself?"

"Nope." George shook his head, then whispered, "We're going to plan B."

George and Shannon had figured out plan B at lunch yesterday. They'd been waiting all week to go back underground—and they couldn't wait any longer. If George's dad didn't leave the house on Saturday, they were going to find a way to sneak down to the basement, anyway. In the daytime.

It was their only chance. George and his dad

were going away to Connecticut to visit George's grandmother that night. And no one was willing to wait until Sunday.

"Okay, plan B," Derrick said softly.

George motioned for Derrick to follow him. For plan B to work, they had to put on a show in front of George's dad.

But when they reached George's room on the second floor, his dad was gone.

George hoped his dad wasn't far away. He assumed he was just up one flight, in his study, with the door open. For their plan to work, he had to be able to hear them.

"So what do you want to do today?" George said loudly.

He and Derrick stood in the hall outside George's room so their voices would carry.

"I don't know. Play video games?" Derrick said. "I got a new one called Mad Ox."

"Cool," George said. "Did you bring it?"

"Uh-uh," Derrick said. "It's at my house."

"Oh, man," George said. "You should have brought it."

"Sorry," Derrick said.

George made a face. *That's not your line!*

Derrick was *supposed* to say, "Let's go over to my house and hang out. We can play the game over there." But he seemed to have forgotten that part.

Come on, George thought. He gestured with his hands, trying to jog Derrick's memory. Derrick shrugged, looking puzzled. His expression said, *What do you want from me?*

George heaved a sigh.

"So I *guess* if we're going to play Mad Ox, we'll have to go hang out at *your* house," he said loudly.

"Oh, yeah," Derrick said with a look of recognition. "Yeah. Right. Let's go to *my* house."

George sighed again. He had to admit, this was pretty clumsy playacting. He hoped it was enough to convince his dad.

He turned and called up the stairs. "Hey, Dad? I'm going over to Derrick's for the day."

A few seconds passed before his dad responded. "What?"

"Is it okay if I spend the day at Derrick's?" George yelled.

"Hold on." George heard his father clomping down the stairs, and finally he reached the landing. "Sorry. I was concentrating on my reading, so I didn't hear you. What did you say?"

All that performance for nothing! George thought.

"I said, is it okay if I spend the day at Derrick's?" George repeated.

"Oh. Yes, fine," his father said. "What time will you be home?"

"I'm not sure," George said. "Can I call you?"

"All right. I have Derrick's number downstairs." His father nodded. Then he gave Derrick a smile. "You must be an awfully good friend to put up with George. You've come all the way over here, and now George wants you to turn around and go back to your house!"

"Yeah, I put up with a lot," Derrick joked.

Mr. van Gelder laughed. "Well, have fun, boys." He turned back toward his study.

"See ya," George called as he and Derrick noisily made their way down the stairs and out the front door.

Out on the street, the two of them walked to the corner without looking back, just in case George's father was watching out the window. As soon as they were out of sight, they gave each other high fives. "Way to go!" Derrick said.

"I can't believe we pulled that off," George agreed. "Hey, any luck with the password?"

Derrick sighed and shook his head. "I've tried everything I can think of. *Leroy, tunnel, subway,* even *Kidd* and *treasure* . . . nothing seems to work."

George gave him a sympathetic look. "Well,

keep trying. Maybe it's just a name, like the name of his wife."

Derrick shrugged. "Maybe. But that could be anything." He frowned and looked around the sidewalk. "Now what?"

"Shannon and Renee are meeting us right here in ten minutes," George said. "Then we sneak back into my house through the window I left open in the basement."

"And hope we don't get caught," Derrick added.

George nodded. "And hope we don't get caught."

Six

Tongue and Eyes

"Does that shirt glow in the dark?" George asked.

He stared at Shannon's T-shirt in the dark basement. He and his friends had just slipped in through the open basement window. Now they were hooking up their climbing gear.

"Yeah," Shannon said. "It's cool, huh? It's one of my parents' tour shirts."

Shannon's parents had been in a rock band in the 1980s. They toured all over Europe, playing sold-out concerts. The T-shirt was black, but the logo was printed with yellowish glow-in-the-dark ink. It had a giant tongue and eyes on the front. The band's name, Raspberry, was on the back.

"I figured with this shirt on, you guys can see me more easily underground," Shannon said.

"True. But so can anyone *else* who's down there," George said nervously.

Shannon shrugged. "I didn't think of that, but really—we've gotten away from Leroy's thugs enough times by now. I'm sure I can just outrun anyone who comes after me."

"Yeah, but you're putting the rest of us in danger, too," Derrick pointed out.

Shannon looked down at her shirt. "Do you really think it's that noticeable?"

"Well, it's too late to change," Renee said. "We're all geared up and ready to go."

Shannon hesitated. "Um . . . maybe I could change into one of George's shirts."

He shook his head. "I can't go upstairs to get you one. My dad's up there."

"You'll be okay," Renee told Shannon, but she didn't sound too sure.

"I have an idea," said Derrick.

Shannon looked at him hopefully.

"Just turn it inside out. That way no glow-in-the-dark tongue and eyes."

Shannon grinned. "Hey, good thinking. All right, you guys—turn around!"

George, Derrick, and Renee all turned to face the wall with the door. George could hear Shannon shuffling around, and then she spoke. "Okay." She grabbed a box to move it away from the secret door. "I'm good to go. I even brought some Oreos for Paul."

The four of them made quick and quiet work of

the trip down. They were really getting to be pros at this. They followed their standard path, marked on the treasure map. Down the streambed. Up the first rock pile. Climb the narrow, angled tunnel.

At the top of the tunnel lay the second pile of rocks—one of Captain Kidd's booby traps that had been sprung a long time ago. Past it, through a small opening, was the old abandoned subway station where they'd first seen Paul.

Shannon was in the lead this time. They flicked off their helmet lights so that she could see if any light was coming from above them. If it was, it meant Leroy's men were back again.

"Anyone up there?" George asked.

"I see a glow," Shannon reported. "Not the big lights, though. More like flickering. It looks like fire."

Fire?

George didn't know what to think about that. What were Leroy's men doing with fire?

They listened hard. George thought he heard voices, but he couldn't be sure.

"Poke your head through the hole," he whispered.

"I am," Shannon answered softly. "Come on up," she called after a minute. "But be quiet."

George hoisted himself up through the opening. Renee and Derrick followed. When they were all standing on the platform, they could see a faint glow from a fire in the distance.

"Down the tracks," Shannon said, pointing. "Remember those shanties we saw when we first met Paul?"

George squinted into the darkness. The glow lit up the shapes of makeshift tents and cardboard boxes where homeless people had been living.

The last time they were there, the shanties had been empty. As if whoever lived in them had left in a hurry.

"Maybe the people who lived there came back," Shannon said. "Maybe they came back when Leroy's men left."

That made sense to George. He had read about homeless people living underground in old subway tunnels and abandoned buildings. They probably moved around a lot. Paul sure did.

"Can we turn on our lights?" Derrick said. "I can't see a thing."

"Not yet," George answered. "Let's creep along the tracks and get a closer look."

The fire in the distance flickered, and George saw some figures moving back and forth in the dim light.

Was one of them Paul? There was only one way to find out.

He took a deep breath and marched forward.

The closer he got to the shanties, the creepier it was. Voices began mumbling down the track.

"Who's there?" a voice said.

"Shadows," another voice said.

"Shadows and sounds. Leroy's playing with us," the first voice said.

"You stay away from us, Leroy!" an old woman's voice called out. She was shouting in George's direction. "Keep your distance, you bully! I've got pepper spray!"

George froze. They'd been spotted, and the tunnel dwellers thought they were Leroy! Suddenly something sailed toward them. A stick or rock. It hit the side of the subway platform.

"Don't!" George called out before he could think better of it.

His heart pounded with fright. But he wasn't going to turn back or quit or run from danger now. Not when they were so close to finding the diamond.

"I'm not Leroy!" George called. "We're just looking for our friend!"

He squinted into the darkness, down the track. The fire was small, not bright enough to make much difference. All he could see were shapes.

No one answered him. In fact, people seemed to be hurrying away. Or hiding in the cardboard tents.

"Turn on your light," Derrick whispered.

"I don't want to scare them," George said. "Maybe they can help us find Paul." George took off his helmet. He cupped his hand over part of the bulb. That way when he flicked it on, it wasn't quite so bright.

"Hello?" George called, letting his light fall toward the shanties.

An old woman stood hunched near a pile of rags and bags, holding a can of something in her hands. Pepper spray, George realized. *Uh-oh.*

She aimed it at George, although he was almost a hundred feet away.

George crouched down. He kept his light trained sideways so it wouldn't be too blinding. He'd already learned from Paul that people who lived underground were very sensitive to the light. He walked toward the woman. The closer he got, the more he could see what was going on by the shanties. It looked like the tunnel dwellers were packing up their little village. They must have come back to get their things now that Leroy was gone, but they weren't going to stay.

"I'm looking for a friend of mine," George called in a friendly voice. "Do you know a boy named Paul?"

Behind the woman there was more movement. Someone carrying a cardboard tent on his back ducked away. A younger woman clanked together a couple of pots and bowls, putting them in a torn plastic bag. George couldn't help but wonder what these people cooked in their pots, what there was to eat down here.

The woman still didn't answer. George crept closer.

"I need to find Paul," George said in a stronger voice. "I'm not working with Leroy, I promise. We just want to find our friend."

When the woman was only fifteen feet in front of him, George stopped. She hadn't budged at all. She still held the can of pepper spray pointing straight at his face.

"Please," George begged. "We have food for him."

The woman made a grumpy-sounding laugh, then turned her back on George. She bent down and pulled some rags around her shoulders. "Fine," she said, her back still turned. "You can do whatever you want in these tunnels—dig anywhere, find your friend Paul. Just don't mess with my home."

George watched the woman curiously. She glanced at George. She had long, matted gray hair and dark eyes. "Down the tracks. Climb into the sewer on the left. Follow the pipes. There's a freshwater stream that makes a waterfall. We go there to drink. He might be there."

"Thank you," George said.

The woman didn't answer.

George motioned for his friends to follow him. One of them—George wasn't sure which—flipped on a helmet light. They needed the light so they could see the sewer.

As they hiked along the track, a rumble started overhead. George jumped before he realized what it was: a working subway train. They were *under* the working subway—that's how deep underground they were. The noise was terrible. Louder, somehow, than if you were standing right beside it. Crumbling bits of the stony ceiling rained down on them as the train roared by.

It made George want to get out of there. Fast.

He turned around to be sure Derrick, Shannon, and Renee were keeping up with him. They were. His three friends—

Wait. Something was wrong.

Behind his three friends George thought he saw another figure. But it was a vague enough shape that he couldn't be sure.

Was it a woman?

Or a shadow?

If it was a woman, was it that same one he thought he'd seen before?

He aimed his light toward the shape.

"Ow!" Derrick complained. "You're blinding me!"

"Sorry," George said. "I just . . . I thought I saw someone back there."

"Who?" Renee turned to look.

"I don't know," George said. "I don't know if it was even really a person. If she was there, she's gone now."

"Weird," muttered Shannon. "Was it a tunnel dweller?"

"I don't know. I thought I saw her the other day, too. But I wasn't sure then, either." George shrugged. "Maybe it's just something weird about the light in this place. Anyway, no one's here now, so we should keep going." He turned around and continued down the tracks.

Finally they spotted the sewer. It was easy to find, from the smell. Too easy.

"Oh, *gross*," said Derrick.

George was glad that there didn't seem to be much liquid in the bottom. They crawled along slowly, trying not to breathe.

At the end of the sewer they spotted a boy hunched down. His clothes were dirty and ragged, and his skin was almost gray from lack of sunlight. He splashed his hands in the water that fell from the natural stream the old woman had described.

"Paul?" George called.

Startled, the boy jerked and ducked.

"Stop the brights!" he pleaded, covering his eyes and pointing to the helmets.

"Turn your light off," George instructed Derrick. But he left his own light on, covered by his cupped hand.

"No brights. I'll go day-blind," Paul complained. He always spoke in simple sentences.

"All right." George sighed and reluctantly switched off the light on his helmet. Immediately the sewer became pitch-black, but George knew that his eyes would adjust in a few minutes. There was a tiny bit of light coming from the opening where the stream emerged. Slowly, his friends and Paul came back into focus.

"You shouldn't be here," Paul warned them. "You don't belong."

George cringed. He knew Paul didn't like them being down there, and yet their whole plan hinged on his being willing to help them.

"Um . . . we brought you something," Shannon said, stepping forward. "Food." She swung off her backpack and rummaged around for a minute. "It's ham and cheese," she said, handing him a sandwich on a big roll.

Paul took the sandwich, sniffed at it, and started devouring it immediately. Greedily. But George thought he saw him wince, as if taking the first bite hurt. *His teeth look pretty scuzzy,* George thought. *People underground probably don't brush very often. Or ever.*

"Hey, Paul, remember the treasure we talked about?" George asked. "And the map I showed you?"

Paul nodded, still chewing.

"We think *you* might know where the treasure is," George said.

Paul barely had any reaction. "Leroy thinks I know," he said. "But I won't tell him."

"*Do* you know?" George asked.

Paul chewed but didn't answer at all.

"Is it in that cave you told me about?" George coaxed. "The one filled with pirate stuff?"

"No." Paul shook his head. "I've looked there."

"But you said there was a skull and crossbones in that cave," Shannon blurted. "I bet it was on a pirate flag. Right?"

"On the wall," Paul said, nodding.

"We need to see that flag," Shannon said. "I think the treasure is behind it. Will you take us there?"

Paul glanced up from the sandwich with a frown. He shook his head. "Why should I help you? You shouldn't be down here."

"Please," Shannon said.

George's stomach was beginning to feel funny again. Was it really the right thing for them to talk

Paul into leading them to the flag room? Should they be trying this shortcut at all?

Paul wouldn't even look at them until he'd finished the sandwich. Then he shook his head again.

"Too many of you," he said. "Leroy will see us."

"*Please,*" Shannon begged. She quickly reached into her backpack and pulled out a plastic bag containing five Oreos. She handed one of the cookies to Paul.

Paul frowned, staring at it suspiciously. "What is it?" he asked.

"It's an Oreo," Renee said. "You know, a cookie."

"Oreo?" Paul sounded puzzled.

He doesn't know what Oreos are, George thought, glancing at his friends. *Maybe he's never even had cookies!*

"It's, um, a special sandwich," Shannon explained quickly. "You eat it after your regular food. It's called a cookie. An Oreo cookie."

Paul looked suspicious, but he took a tiny bite. Immediately his face spread into a smile. He popped the rest of it into his mouth whole.

"*Mmm,*" he mumbled, chewing. He glanced at the rest of the cookies in Shannon's bag. Shannon held them away from him.

"You know, you can have *all* of these," she said,

glancing at George. "But only if you promise to take us to the pirate cave."

Paul frowned. He looked at the Oreos, then at Shannon. He seemed to be considering his options.

"If I take you," he said, "you can't come back. When you have what you're looking for, you go. For good. And you have to be quiet. And careful. And not use brights when I tell you not to."

George looked around at his friends. Paul's conditions seemed pretty reasonable. "All right," he said simply.

"Sure," Derrick echoed.

"Fine with me," said Renee.

"Yeah," Shannon agreed.

Paul glanced at all of them in turn, then reached out and grabbed the Oreos from Shannon. He ripped open the bag and shoved two cookies in his mouth.

"That's it for now," Shannon said. "I keep the last two until you get us to the cave."

Paul looked down at the Oreos in his hand, frowned, and then handed them back to Shannon without a word. She took the ripped-up bag and stuck it in her pocket.

"Let's go," Paul said, his mouth full.

Seven

Rats

The trip to the pirate cave took almost a whole hour, by George's watch.

Most of the route was rough going. They had to crawl on all fours through two natural tunnels carved by streams. Then Paul led them through a metal grate that opened into the basement of an abandoned building teeming with rats. Only a thin shaft of light from a high, dirty basement window lit up the space.

George's pulse doubled when he saw the rodents scurrying around on the basement floor.

Don't tell me you're leading us there.

"Forget it," Shannon said, shaking her head.

The five of them lingered by the open grate, waiting to jump down to the floor.

"Throw stones at them," Paul instructed.

"No way." Derrick shook his head. "I'm *not* going down there."

Paul threw a few small rocks. The rats skittered to the corners, but they were still down there.

"Isn't there another way to get to the pirate cave?" Shannon asked.

"Not today," Paul said. "Leroy's men are there."

"In the pirate cave?" George's voice raised in desperation. "They're beating us to the treasure?"

"No. They're digging in the tunnel I mostly use," Paul said. "We can't go the easy way."

Shannon took a deep breath, watching the rats. "Where are we going after we jump down to that basement floor?" she asked Paul.

He pointed toward a hole on the far side of the room where the wall had crumbled away.

"But the rats are going *in* there!" Derrick objected.

"The crawlers aren't bad," Paul said. "They come here to get water from a pipe that leaks. They only bite if you have food in your pockets."

Shannon jerked back, bumping her head on the roof of the tunnel. Luckily she was wearing her helmet. "Uh-oh. I've still got two Oreos left," she said.

"Give them to me," George said.

"Huh?" Shannon said.

George held out his hand. "Give me the cookies."

Shannon did. George broke them into several pieces and tossed them down to the basement floor.

"Hey!" Paul cried. "No fair!"

George had thrown the cookies into the far corner, away from the opening where they needed to go. Immediately the rats swarmed toward the food.

"Listen, we'll bring you more Oreos next time, I promise," George said. "Come on—let's go while the rats are busy."

Not waiting for an answer, George jumped down first. Then Paul. Then the other three. George darted over to the opening, turning to steal a quick glance at the rats before he followed Paul through. They were busy with the Oreos, but George felt his skin crawl at being so close to them. They had grimy, matted fur, fat pink tails, and bulging red eyes. George shuddered, but what choice did he have? He *had* to find that pirate cave. Even if the treasure wasn't buried with the Jolly Roger, maybe one of the other maps *was.*

Quickly all five of them ducked into the small hole in the opposite basement wall. It was pitch-black inside.

"Ew, ew, ew," said Shannon. "I hope I never have to do that again."

"How do you think we're getting back?" asked Derrick.

"Ooooooh." George could hear Shannon shudder. "Well, I'm not going to think about that."

George flicked on his helmet light and shielded it with his hand, so only a faint ray of light trickled onto the tunnel wall.

Amazingly, he could stand up. And there were steps inside! Old stone steps, going down. They looked like they were two hundred years old, at least. Paul led the way.

At the bottom of the steps was another stream. A bigger one.

"I wonder what this was in the old days," George muttered. From the look of it, the stream might have once been a river. Maybe those steps led down from someone's house a long time ago. Maybe there had been a boat launch at the bottom.

The water was cold, but Paul showed them where they could walk on rocks so their feet only got slightly wet. George let his helmet light scan the tunnel. It was completely different from the other tunnels they had explored. There was no trash. No graffiti. Nothing about Leroy. No one living here. This place was totally and completely removed from civilization.

"Hey, Paul," he said, "does anyone else ever come down here? I mean, the people who live near the subway station . . . or Leroy?"

Paul shook his head, stepping up onto a rock. "Never," he said. "There's nothing down here for them."

Good! George thought. *Then maybe we'll really be the first to find the treasure!*

Except . . .

George's stomach still felt all squiggly. There was something wrong with this shortcut—something that didn't make sense and could throw off their whole plan. In a flash, George remembered. *Leroy and his men are digging. Leroy's men tied Paul up and questioned him. Paul gave them something they wanted, and now they are digging.*

"Paul," George said. "What did you tell Leroy's men? What did you *give* them?"

Paul was quiet.

"Was it a map? Did it have something to do with a Jolly Roger?" George asked.

"What's a Jolly Roger?" Paul replied, a little defensively.

"The flag—the pirate flag you said was in the cave," George explained.

Paul shook his head, but he didn't say anything more.

"So what *was* it?" George asked finally. "We know you gave them something. We heard Leroy's men talking about it."

"What does it matter?" Paul turned around and gave George a challenging look.

"Why should we trust you if you won't tell us what you gave Leroy?" George asked. "Maybe you know more about the treasure maps than you told us. Maybe you're working for Leroy now."

Derrick glanced over and gave George a "fat chance" look. George knew it wasn't likely, but there was something weird about the way Paul was acting.

Paul shrugged and looked away. "It was a funny rock I found," he said finally. "It had letters and stuff on it. I don't know what it was."

"Letters and stuff?" Shannon piped up. "What kind of letters?"

"I dunno." Paul was walking really fast now down the tunnel. He was already a good ten feet ahead of them.

"Would you recognize the letters if you saw them again?" Derrick asked. "Maybe we could write out an alphabet, and you could show us the letters you recognize."

Paul turned around and scowled. "They all look the same to me," he said. "Besides, I didn't get a good look at them."

George glanced at his friends. *Maybe we should drop it,* he thought. Paul didn't seem to want to talk about it, and they could all talk about what they thought it was later, when the four of them were alone. He shook his head ever so slightly, and Derrick nodded. Shannon and Renee both gave George looks to let him know they understood.

They walked along for a few minutes with nobody saying anything.

"That's a weird name for a flag," Paul said finally. "Jolly Roger? You use different words on the dayside."

Derrick laughed. "Hey, I think it's a weird name, too. Where did that name come from, anyway? Some pirate named Roger?"

"Nope." George was happy to have a chance to show off his knowledge of pirate lore. "Most experts think it's from a French phrase—*joli rouge*—which means 'beautiful red.'"

"Beautiful red what? I thought the Jolly Roger was a *black* flag," Renee said.

"It is," George explained. "The red flag was this special signal that pirates and other ships used. If a ship with a red flag flying approached another ship at sea, it meant the captain wouldn't take prisoners. He would kill anyone on the other ship who resisted. The red flag was the *joli rouge*."

"The *joli rouge*?" Renee asked.

"Yeah. And people who didn't speak French thought they were saying Jolly Roger," George said. "Some other people think Jolly Roger comes from Old Roger—which is a British name for the devil."

"Okay," said Shannon as they continued through the tunnel. "So that explains why they would call a red flag 'Jolly Roger.' But why did they start calling the black flag with a skull and crossbones by that name?"

"Well," said George, "in pirate times ships always flew *some* kind of flag to let other ships know who they were. Usually it was the flag of their country. But if the crew got sick with a deadly disease like the black plague, they put up a black flag with a skull and crossed bones on it."

"Oh, that's cool," Renee said. "I get it. It was like a warning to stay away? So the other ships' crews wouldn't get the plague?"

"Right," George said. "But then pirate ships caught on and started using it as a trick, just to keep other ships away. I mean, the pirates didn't want anyone else coming on board and stealing the loot they'd already stolen."

"Pretty sneaky," Shannon said, sounding impressed.

"So," George continued, "by that time people were using the phrase 'Jolly Roger' to mean any kind of pirate flag. And eventually people started to recognize that the skull and crossbones meant 'pirate' instead of 'plague.' So that's how the skull and crossbones flag got the name."

"What's a pirate?" Paul asked.

"It's a person who steals from another person. Usually on a ship, on the ocean," George explained.

Paul was silent. George wasn't sure whether he knew what a ship was. Or the ocean.

For the next few minutes they walked in silence.

Finally, they reached a break in the stone wall. A natural cave. "This is it," Paul told them.

George felt his skin tingling in anticipation.

The opening was only about three feet wide and less than three feet high. They had to crouch down and almost crawl on their bellies to get in.

But once they were inside the cave, they could stand up. And the ceiling was high! The cave was about the size of a small bedroom. And George could see that Paul was right—it was *full* of old pirate stuff. So full, it was difficult to see just what was there. Nothing looked like treasure, but who knew?

They took off their helmets and put them on the ground, pointing up, so the light wouldn't be blinding anyone.

"Cool!" Shannon said, kneeling to touch an old, moldy, blue sea captain's coat.

It was lying on the stone floor of the cave straight in front of them. The wool had been eaten by mice in about twenty places, and some of the brass buttons were missing. The ones that remained were dull with tarnish, but the coat still had its gold braid at the shoulders. It was clearly an ancient piece of clothing, but there was a certain magic about it. "Being in the cave all these years must have preserved it," George murmured to himself.

Lying beside the coat was a black broad-brimmed hat.

George walked toward them as if in a trance.

This was it: what he'd been looking for his whole life. Something belonging to Captain Kidd. Somehow, even more than the journal, this seemed real. A captain's coat and hat. The ones actually worn by Kidd—who had been married to George's great-times-eight grandmother. He felt like, by finding this wonderful treasure, he was somehow getting closer to his own mother. To something she had cared about.

He bent down, picked up the hat, and put it on.

"How do I look?" he said, turning to show his friends.

And that's when he saw it. The Jolly Roger—it was hanging on the wall of the cave behind him, over the entrance.

Shannon and Derrick turned to follow his gaze and spotted it, too. Without missing a beat they started moving toward it, reaching up to pull it down.

Wait! said George. Or maybe he didn't say it. Maybe he only heard it in his mind. In a flash, he knew that something was terribly wrong. And his friends were going to suffer for their mistake—they all might suffer.

"*Stop!*" George shouted at the top of his lungs. "Don't touch it! *Don't*!"

Eight

TRAPS

"What's wrong?" Shannon cried, frozen. Her hands were still in the air, reaching for the flag.

"Don't touch it!" George repeated, his eyes wide. "Don't even move!"

He looked up at the ceiling. The ceiling was high and the cave was dark, so it was difficult to make out what he was looking for. But he could see the shadow of something when he squinted. He had the sickening feeling that his premonition had been right. And they had come so close to touching the flag!

"I need a stick," he announced, scanning the floor of the cave.

He didn't see a stray branch anywhere. *Of course not,* George thought. There *were* no sticks underground. Sticks came from trees. Nothing was growing down here in the dark.

Renee removed a rope and carabiner—part of her climbing gear—from a clip on her belt. The carabiner was a heavy, oval-shaped hook.

"How about this?" she asked, handing them to George.

"Yeah, these might work," George said. "Thanks."

It wasn't a stick, but the rope was long enough. He just had to aim it very carefully. He scanned the ceiling of the cave again, then pointed to the back corner. Away from the flag. Away from the opening to the cave.

"Stand back there," he told his friends. Then he swung the rope and carabiner like a lasso, trying to knock the Jolly Roger down. On his second try the carabiner caught the edge of the flag and pulled it away from the wall. For one moment George could see how the trap was put together: The flag was held in place by a kind of leather pulley, which connected to an iron hook in the ceiling, which moved slightly to the left. . . .

There was a loud *crack* from above, like a piece of wood snapping.

"Look out!" George yelled, jumping back to join his friends in the corner.

As he jumped, the whole cave seemed to explode with sound. The ceiling opened, releasing a huge boulder—it was almost the size of a car! The wind it created sent their hair flying back. The boulder landed on the cave floor with a deafening sound. The floor beneath them shook with the impact. To George, it felt like the whole city must be shaking.

"Holy *cow!*" Derrick yelled. "We would have been pancakes!"

"Oh my gosh," Shannon said, trembling. "It was booby-trapped!"

"How did you *know*?" Renee asked George.

"I didn't really," George admitted. "Something's been bothering me since we got the clue. It's like it all snapped into place just now. Captain Kidd didn't think of himself as a pirate—he was a privateer. He had a license from the king to prey on the king's enemies. So he would never, ever sail under a pirate's flag."

"So you figured the Jolly Roger had to be a trap?" Derrick asked.

George nodded. "*Eternal* reward—it could mean you get what you deserve. And if you got killed by a falling boulder, well, that would be eternal."

"Wow." It was all Shannon could say—and all she *had* to say. George grinned at the compliment.

Even Paul looked impressed.

"For someone from the dayside, you know a lot about the caves," Paul said.

"I know a lot about Captain Kidd," George said with a modest shrug. "I guess because he's sort of a family member. By marriage, I mean."

"Well, if you're so smart, tell me this," Paul said. "How are we going to get out of here?"

Out? George took in a sharp breath. Uh-oh.

George had been so happy about not being crushed by the booby trap, he hadn't even noticed that the fallen boulder was now blocking the opening. They were trapped.

"Oh, man," Derrick said, rushing to see if Paul was right.

But it was true. The boulder had fallen straight down in front of the cave's opening.

Thanks a lot, Kidd! George thought in frustration. George kept trying to defend Kidd in his mind, but he had to admit the privateer was pretty ruthless.

George looked around the cave again. Suddenly it seemed a lot smaller than it had when they'd first found it. He tried to picture the five of them wasting away in this secret place . . . sleeping under the pirate flag . . . desperately chewing on the wool coat, just like mice. They wouldn't last more than a week without water, and their bodies would waste away to skeletons, to be found by some other young band of treasure hunters three hundred years in the future. . . .

"Can we move it?" Shannon said. George snapped back to reality and felt his spirits lifting a little. Maybe there was hope. Shannon hurried to give the boulder a push. With all her weight behind her, she leaned into it.

"Ow," she said. "It's *way* heavy."

"It'll take all of us," Derrick said. "Come on. Everyone get on this side. Then we'll all shove together."

Derrick and George bent into position. They stood shoulder to shoulder, ready to push. Renee and Shannon were on either side. Paul was the weakest—or at least he looked weak—so they had him take an end.

"On the count of three," George said. "One . . . two . . . three!"

The huge stone rocked slightly, but it was flat on the bottom. It wouldn't roll over. When they stopped pushing, it settled back where it had started.

"Oh, man. We're trapped!" Derrick moaned. "We're going to die."

"Try the walkie-talkies?" Shannon said to Renee.

"But I have both of them," Renee answered, shaking her head. "They never worked very well in the tunnels. And now there's no one to answer us."

"Trapped," Derrick repeated.

Okay, stay cool, George told himself. *Try to think. There are five of us here. We ought to be able to move that boulder somehow.*

But panic was beginning to rise in his throat.

What if they *couldn't* get out? What if they were trapped in there forever? They'd die, and no one would ever find them.

Because no one ever came down this tunnel.

Ever.

Nine

PROMISES MADE

"I have an idea," Shannon said suddenly.

"Does it involve sending out for a pizza?" Derrick joked. "I'm starved."

"Pizza?" Paul said the word as if he'd never heard it before.

"It's a kind of food we have on the dayside," George explained. "What's your idea, Shannon?" He'd be grateful for any kind of hope at this point.

"Help me with this rope," Shannon said. She picked up the long length of rope and the carabiners they used for climbing. Quickly she fastened the rope around the boulder in several directions. She left a long tail sticking out of one side, toward the back of the cave.

"This is how they moved the stones for the pyramids," Shannon said. "At least, that's what I read once."

"Cool!" Derrick said. "Everyone grab onto the rope and pull."

"No." Renee shook her head. "Shannon and

Paul and I will pull. You and George stand on the other side. When we get it rocking, you guys push it over."

"On the count of three!" George said.

The girls and Paul grunted and pulled hard. Very slowly the boulder began to move. First it lifted just a tiny bit, but they pulled on the rope even harder, and soon the boulder was rocking back and forth, rising a few inches out of its rest.

"Almost!" George cried.

The girls and Paul kept pulling. Little by little the boulder moved farther and farther out of its spot. Finally, George and Derrick placed their hands on the other side of the boulder, at the same time the girls and Paul were pulling, and pushed with all their might.

There was a creaking sound as the boulder rubbed against the hard ground. Then all at once the rock rolled over, out of the way.

"*Yes!*" Shannon cheered, running over with Renee to give high fives to the boys.

George and Derrick whooped and laughed. George couldn't believe how great he felt. He had been completely convinced he'd never leave that cave again, and now they were free to go.

"Nice teamwork!" Shannon said.

Then George realized something.

Someone was missing. *Paul!*

"Hey—where did Paul go?" George asked.

Derrick, Shannon, and Renee looked around. But it was obvious: Paul was no longer in the cave.

"He was just here," Shannon muttered, baffled.

"Well, we'd better find him," Renee said, craning her neck to look out the opening. "Maybe he just needed some air."

Quickly the four of them put on their helmets and scampered out of the cave. George went last so he could bring Captain Kidd's coat with him. As an afterthought he grabbed the pirate flag, too, which had fallen to the ground. Maybe he would want to remember this someday.

"Paul?" The four of them looked around the streambed. "Hey—*wait!*" Shannon suddenly started running, and George looked where she was headed.

Sure enough, there was Paul, about forty feet away, running like crazy and not looking back.

"Wait!" Shannon called again. "Don't leave us here! We don't know the way back!"

Paul stopped. He turned around, squinting and shielding his eyes from the bright beams of their helmet lights.

"Don't you get it? You don't belong down here," he said simply.

George took off his helmet and aimed the light

sideways. "I know," he agreed. "We don't. But we've got to find the treasure. And you can help."

"No, it's too late." Paul answered. "You'll never find it. Leroy is ahead of you."

George frowned. So Leroy was looking for the treasure. But why? How? They were the ones with the map and the journal—not him. George felt like there was too much information to keep track of, but something didn't seem right. "Don't be so sure," he said. "We found a book—a journal. It belonged to Captain Kidd. And it has lots of clues."

He hesitated, wondering if Paul even knew what a book was.

"Clues?" Paul asked.

"Yes," George said. "They tell us how to find the other treasure maps. There are four of them."

"Four?" Paul's eyes lit up, as though something was making a lot of sense. He walked back toward them.

"That's right," George said. "We have to figure out what the clues mean. And then maybe you can help us find the other maps. You know your way around down here, and we don't."

"And we'll share the treasure with you," Shannon reminded him.

"I want more Oreos," Paul said matter-of-factly.

"Oh! Of course!" Shannon said. "I'll bring you some as soon as I can. I *promise*."

"How many?" Paul asked.

"A whole bag," Shannon said.

"How many is that?" Paul asked.

"I don't know. Thirty?" she said.

"Two bags," he said plainly.

"Deal," Shannon agreed quickly. "Okay, now that we know that pirate cave was just a trap, should we figure out how to find the other maps?"

Definitely, George thought. They were wasting precious time. He had to return home by five o'clock so he and his dad could go visit his grandmother.

"I think we should make a pact," George said. "That we stick to finding the rest of the maps and don't take any more shortcuts."

"Right on," Derrick agreed. "I don't want to die in some abandoned cave with creepy pirate junk."

George looked at the two girls. Renee nodded, and Shannon bit her lip.

"You're right," she said with a sigh. "I'm sorry I led us down here. I just got so excited about finding the treasure right away."

"I know," George assured her. "I mean, we were all pretty excited. But now that I think about it, why *would* Captain Kidd have a real shortcut to the treasure? He wanted whoever found that treasure to be worthy of it. We can't just stumble onto the treasure—we have to *earn* it."

"And we will," Renee said with a grin. "First we have to figure out how to find map two."

"Let's go back to the clues," George said, thinking out loud. "The last one said, 'If you seek eternity, you must snatch nine lives from a dead man's hand.'"

"I saw a dead man down here once," Paul said.

How awful, George thought. He had never seen anyone dead. And he didn't want to.

"Well," said George, taking a deep breath, "all we know is that we need to find a corpse. It would only be a skeleton by now. Paul, the dead man you saw—was it like that? Was he just a skeleton?"

Paul frowned, like he didn't want to think about it. "He was just a pile of bones. But smiling. Like this." He pressed his teeth together and gave a big, gruesome smile, like you would see on a skull. "I can show you where he is. If he's still down there. I don't go there much anymore."

George nodded excitedly. "Yeah, Paul, please take us there."

Paul sighed and led the way. They followed him down the stream and up the stairs. There they stood for a minute in front of the hole in the wall, looking into the rat-filled basement.

"Ugh," said Shannon.

"Wait, I just remembered something." Derrick

dug his hand into his jeans pocket, frowning. "Yup . . . there they are." He pulled out his hand and revealed a half-eaten roll of cherry Life Savers. "Do you think rats like Life Savers?"

"The crawlers like anything with a smell," Paul put in. He picked a piece of candy off the top of the roll and quickly sniffed it. "Smells like sugar. The crawlers will like this." He looked uncertainly at the candy, frowning.

"Go ahead, try it," said Derrick.

Paul carefully plopped the Life Saver on his tongue. He bit down and made a face. George and his friends could hear the loud *crunch*.

"Wait, don't chew it," Shannon advised. "Just kind of hold it in your mouth and suck on it."

Paul did as Shannon said and slowly began to smile. "Sweet," he said.

"All right, Derrick," George said, peering out at the rats. "Just throw a couple of candies out there, and hopefully they'll all go for it."

Derrick pulled out a couple more Life Savers, aimed, and tossed them across the room. A few rats stayed where they were, but most ran over to investigate.

"I guess this is as good as it gets," George said. "Let's go!"

As fast as they could, all five of them scurried out

of the opening, across the room, and up through the grate. They just barely got Shannon through before the rats started sniffing at her feet. Back in the tunnel Shannon sighed. "Phew! That was too close."

"Now where?" George asked Paul. "Where'd you see the skeleton?"

"It's down this way," Paul replied. "But through a different tunnel."

He led them about twenty feet down the stream, then pointed out a small opening in the left wall.

"You have to be quiet now," Paul said. "Turn out the brights."

Once again they crawled into a small space in nearly complete darkness.

Then the tunnel turned.

Past the bend, there wasn't even a shred of light. George couldn't see a thing—not shapes, not outlines of the walls, not even his hand in front of his face. He breathed in nervously, with no idea what lay ahead of them. He felt completely helpless.

"Can you see in here?" George asked Paul.

"No," Paul admitted. "Not now. But it's only a short tunnel."

Moving slowly, George and his friends shuffled along behind Paul.

"Do you know this tunnel well?" Shannon asked. George could hear the concern in her voice.

Paul didn't answer for a few seconds. "I know it okay," he said finally. "I haven't been down here in a long time."

"But you're sure that it's short?" George asked. He tried to look around but saw nothing but blackness. "Paul, if you you're not sure where you're going, maybe I should be in front. I'm the captain."

"The what?"

"I'm the—the leader, sort of. Trust me." George could hear that his friends had stopped, and he carefully felt his way ahead, passing Shannon, Derrick, Renee, and finally Paul. He put his arms out on either side, feeling the walls of the tunnel. Carefully, he stepped forward.

"All right, guys," he said, hoping he sounded more confident than he felt. "Let's go."

Slowly the five of them made their way farther down the tunnel. George could see that it wasn't getting any brighter—they weren't even close to the end. "Was the dead guy in this tunnel, Paul?" he asked, feeling his way along the wall. "Or was he somewhere—"

Suddenly he felt his toe smack into something hard in the floor. Without any warning, he pitched forward.

"Yahhh!"

He desperately used his arms to search the

space in front of him for something to grab onto. But there was nothing. He couldn't see the walls of the tunnel, and he had no idea where he was falling. He flailed aimlessly, hoping to use his arms to catch himself when he fell.

"Ahhh!" George felt himself doubling over, about to land flat on his face on the rocky floor. His first thought was that this was going to be pretty painful. There was nothing to hold on to to slow himself down, and the ground in this tunnel was all uneven and sharp. And his second thought was that he was in bigger trouble than that.

Because there *wasn't* any ground in front of him. He went straight through the tunnel floor falling facefirst—into who knew what!

Ten
Falling

"AAAAAAHHHHH!"

George screamed as he plunged through the floor and felt himself fall into nothingness. He flailed around. It was too dark to see how far he was falling or what he would land in. George could feel his heart lurch up into his throat. It was the most terrifying feeling he'd ever experienced.

"George!" cried Shannon.

Just then he felt himself land in something. Not on something—*in* something. It was like water, but it was more sludgy than wet. *I'm still alive,* thought George. *I landed somewhere, and I'm not dead yet!*

It was definitely a start.

"George—what *happened*?"

A light flicked on above George's head, and suddenly he could see the walls of the cave around him. He tried to move and get a look at what he had fallen into. He could see that he was in a small space about ten feet below the tunnel. Then all at once he began to feel himself sinking. The panic

that had just dissolved suddenly seized his whole
body again. *Sinking!* He looked up and saw
Shannon's face peering through the hole he'd fallen
through. What was he in? He felt like he was sinking
in a lake, but the water felt gritty—he moved his fingers through the—

"Quicksand!" George screamed, panic coursing
through his veins. "I'm sinking! I'm sinking! I don't
know how deep this is!" He thrashed around, trying
to grab onto something—anything! In the movies
wasn't there always a tree nearby? But there wasn't
going to be a tree in the tunnels! He was doomed.
"Help me, guys!"

"George, stay calm!" George looked up again and
saw that Renee's face had replaced Shannon's in the
opening. "Stay calm and stay *still*. It's thrashing
around that makes you sink faster. What you have
to do is stay still. People can float on quicksand!"

George heard what Renee was saying, but it
didn't seem right to him somehow. He had to
force himself to stop moving his arms and legs. It
didn't feel natural. Slowly he realized that he was
no longer sinking. He tried to take a deep breath
and relax. But that didn't seem possible.

"Let's get you out of there." Renee began lowering the rope they'd used to move the boulder.
"You're going to have to grab this and attach it to

your carabiner. Move very slowly. No thrashing!"

George watched the rope lower down. He tried to move his arm out of the quicksand, but it was hard. It was like the quicksand had him in a vacuum hold. Finally his arm was released with a loud *smack*! The rope landed just a few feet in front of him. Carefully George moved one leg, then the other. He "swam" through the thick grit until he was just close enough to grab the rope.

The carabiner was attached to his climbing harness. He had to thread the rope through the loop and knot it. Moving as little as possible, George leaned back, so he could reach the carabiner at his waist without submerging his hand back in the quicksand. George's hands, sticky and numb, fumbled with the rope until it was securely tied.

"Okay!" he called.

Renee looked down. "Try to get as much of you out of the quicksand as possible," she instructed. "Try to kind of float on it, on your back."

George then heard a chorus of grunts from his friends. They were trying to pull him up. He was raised a few inches, but the sand had a tight hold on his legs. It seemed to work like a suction cup, holding him down there.

"*UUURRGHH!*" he heard his friends yell as they pulled harder.

Smack!

All at once the quicksand released its hold and George was free. He bounced a little in the air over the quicksand, then grabbed tighter onto the rope and tried to climb up a little.

Slowly George was pulled up through the air until he was close enough to grab the edges of the hole. His friends gave one last yank, and he gripped the sides of the opening and heaved himself out. He lay on the floor for a moment, gasping. The rock floor of the tunnel felt like heaven. Solid ground!

"Are you okay?" Derrick asked. "How did you fall? I don't understand."

George had the impulse to shrug, but he was too exhausted even for that. "I don't know. I tripped on something, and I fell forward. The next thing I knew, the floor just dropped away!"

His friends immediately looked around the tunnel with their helmet lights. Shannon reached her hands into the hole, feeling around. "There's a trapdoor!" she cried.

All five of them crouched down to look, and sure enough—an ancient-looking wooden door, about two feet wide and four feet long, hung just below the opening. "It must be a booby trap," George said. "We don't have a map for this part of the tunnels. We didn't have any warning."

"I think I've figured it out," said Derrick, still looking around the tunnel. "This rock you tripped on—it looks like it's attached to a rusty lever. When you stumbled, you triggered the trapdoor to open and fell right through!"

"Great," muttered George. "That Captain Kidd, whatta guy." George knew that his sort-of ancestor had only been trying to protect his treasure, but *come on*. This was getting ridiculous.

"Sorry, George." Suddenly Paul was standing over him. "The brights hurt my eyes in little tunnels. I didn't know there were traps in here. I would have let you use them if I had."

George nodded. "It's okay, Paul." He dragged himself to his feet. He was covered in gritty, sticky mud. "You didn't know."

"Are you all right?" Shannon looked him up and down, like she was making sure all his arms and legs were still there. "I would have freaked out if that had happened to me! You must have been terrified!"

George shrugged. "It wasn't fun." He tried to brush some of the sand off his clothes, but it stuck to him like it was mixed with superglue.

"There must be natural springs under these tunnels," Renee suggested. "I read in your *New York Underground* book that all you need to make quicksand is water and sand. It happens a lot in damp, marshy places. Like Manhattan used to be, before the city was built. Quicksand was one of the biggest dangers when they were building the subways."

"Leave it to Captain Kidd to use it as a booby trap," Derrick said. "Guys, we have to be careful when we're walking through tunnels we don't have a map for."

Shannon nodded. "Maybe we should turn back now."

"No." George shook his head furiously. The quicksand had been really scary, but he had to be brave. And he was feeling a lot better now that he was out of it and everyone had their lights on. "I didn't go through all that for nothing. Let's find that dead guy! And the diamond!"

Before his friends could respond, George started walking. This time he turned on his helmet light so he could see what was in front of him. After a few steps he heard his friends behind him.

They had been walking a few minutes when, very gradually, George sensed light entering the tunnel. Finally the tunnel turned again and he could see the opening. When they came out, they were in a huge cave with what looked like a domed ceiling. Gray daylight streamed in from a small opening at the far end.

George smelled a mixture of river, sewer, and something else. Something really *awful*.

I know that smell, he thought, remembering his aunt's cat's litter box.

And no wonder.

As soon as his eyes adjusted to the light, George saw that the place was *crawling* with cats. Not just normal cats, but scrawny wild cats, coming and going through the small opening. Everywhere. They were mangy and feral looking. As an orange cat passed on George's left, George could see he was missing an eye and part of his ear.

"Look out!" Derrick said, dodging a rat that sprang out of nowhere and ran past his foot.

George jumped and Shannon let out a yelp. "Yuck! They're *following* us!" she cried.

Almost instantly three or four of the hissing cats pounced on the rodent. One grabbed the rat's ear, one grabbed the rat's tail, and one clamped his teeth right over its midsection. The cats yowled, and the one with the tail reached out to claw one of the others on the nose. None of the cats wanted to let the rat go, and they began to fight viciously over it.

"They come for the crawlers," Paul said.

"Oh, gross," Shannon cried as the cats began to pull the rat apart. "This is disgusting."

"No kidding," George agreed. He had thought he was getting used to being underground, but these cats were creepier than anything he'd ever seen.

George took a step forward, trying to get away from the cat who had "won" the rat and was proceeding to devour it. But in his haste to get away, he accidentally stepped on the tail of a big black tomcat. The cat whirled around and let out an ear-piercing *"YEOOOOOOWWWLLL!"* and then arched his back and hissed at George, swiping at his legs with a huge black paw. George could feel the claws scraping his skin even through his jeans. "Owww!" he cried, carefully stepping back to avoid both the tomcat and the rat eater.

"I don't see any dead man," Derrick said nervously. "Let's get out of here."

"No, wait," George insisted. "Paul saw a dead man in here. We have to check it out. Paul, where was he?"

"He's probably been eaten by these cats," Derrick grumbled.

Paul looked around. "I told you I haven't been here in a long time," he said. "But I think he was over there." He pointed to a far wall that had a tiny opening at the bottom. Cats passed in and out easily, but George and his friends would have to crawl through on their bellies.

"What were you doing crawling through there?" George asked as they walked over to the opening, dodging cats.

"Running from Leroy." Paul shrugged. "It was a couple of years ago."

George shook his head. He could never get his mind around the kind of life Paul led—being chased by thugs, squeezing into strange caves only to come face-to-face with a grinning skeleton. George was having a hard time handling all this adventure now. He couldn't imagine having to do it when he was only a little kid.

"I'll go first," Shannon offered, getting down on her hands and knees. "I sure hope there aren't any rats in here." She poked her head into the opening, then shimmied through until only her sneakers remained. "Oh my gosh. Cool! You guys won't believe this."

"I'll go next," said Renee, and one by one she, Derrick, and George squeezed through the opening. Paul went last. George guessed he was in no hurry to see the dead man again.

On the other side of the opening George stood up and looked around. They were in another whole room! Or rather, a cave: a long, narrow chamber. Shannon and Renee were already stepping forward. George took a look at what lay ahead of them and gasped.

"Don't move!" he commanded them sharply. "Look! The whole thing is a giant booby trap!"

Eleven

Dead Man's Hand

All four of the pyrates stood staring into the cave. Behind them Paul squeezed through and stood up.

"Whoa," Derrick said, letting out a low whistle. "Check out those knives!"

"Cutlasses," George corrected him.

"Whatever," Derrick said.

A few feet in front of them swung two cutlasses—huge pirate swords with curved blades. One hung down from the ceiling. The other was mounted on a wooden board that stuck up from the ground. They were connected somehow—George could see that much.

And the vibrations from the five of them entering the cave had started the cutlasses swinging back and forth.

"This is wild," Renee said breathlessly.

"The treasure must be in here!" Shannon exclaimed. "Otherwise why would Kidd protect it so well?"

"Oh, man, there he is," Renee said, pointing ahead. "The *dead* man!"

Renee was right. At the far end was a skeleton. And in his hand was an old, frayed whip—a carved wooden handle that led out to nine separate strands of leather.

"What's in his hand?" Shannon asked. "And what does it have to do with nine lives?"

"It's a cat-o'-nine-tails," George replied. "I've read about them in the books my dad gave me; the pirates liked them. It's a special kind of whip. See how it has those nine long pieces of leather? Because the whip has nine cords, each lashing gives you nine times the hurt."

"That's it," Derrick said. "That cat-o'-nine-tails must be what the clue meant. We have to take the whip from his hand."

George shivered. He was thinking that this hadn't been a skeleton when Captain Kidd put it there. No way.

It had been a *corpse*!

George stared at the skeleton, wondering who the man had been and hoping that he had done something really horrible to inspire Kidd to kill him. He made a mental note to search the journal for some kind of clue.

"Maybe the map is in the handle of the whip," George said, still not moving.

"Whoa!" Derrick said, watching the swinging

blades. "No way anyone can get past those things."

It would be difficult, George realized. You'd have to duck first, or else your head would be chopped off! Then you'd have to jump to avoid having your legs cut off.

Beyond the sharp blades he could see some hurdles built out of stone. And past those George saw a plank, something like a ship's gangplank.

Slowly, one careful step at a time, he moved forward.

"Check out that gangplank," he said, shining his light at it. "It stretches out over the edge of a pit."

His friends took two steps forward, following his light. They all stared.

At the end of the plank, just overhead, a rope dangled.

"It looks like if you grab that rope, you can swing the rest of the way across the pit and reach the other side," Renee said. The pit looked to be about fifteen feet wide in all.

"Maybe *you* could," George shot back. "I don't know about me."

"But you have to get over the pit to get to the skeleton," Shannon said.

"Okay. Who's going to go?" Derrick asked.

"I will," both Renee and Shannon said at once.

George felt scared, but he wanted to be brave. And he didn't want his friends to get hurt. Captain Kidd set this trap, and George felt responsible.

"I will," he said finally. "I mean, I *should*, because I'm the captain."

Renee looked doubtful. "Thanks for offering, George. And you *are* our captain. But I still think I should go. I have more experience climbing and stuff."

Paul, who had been quiet this whole time, now stepped forward.

"No, *I* should do it," he said. "I'm fast, and I'm used to crawling around down here, in small places. And I can see better than any of you in the dark."

There was silence for a minute. Everyone looked at George, waiting for him to decide.

"It's between Paul and Renee," George said finally. "They are the most athletic."

Paul and Renee looked at each other. "I'm going," Renee said suddenly, and took off without waiting another moment.

She turned toward the narrow chamber and took a deep breath.

The cutlasses were swinging slowly. But every time a cat darted into the space and the air moved, they swung a little faster. It was going to be tough to judge when to run through.

"Be careful!" Shannon called.

But it was too late. Renee was already ducking under the first sword, then leaping over the second.

The blade from the second cutlass whizzed past her boots, just barely missing her. George could feel his heart pounding in his chest. "You can do it, Renee!"

She leaped over a pile of stones and landed with a thud on something wooden—something out of sight on the far side of the rock pile.

Another booby trap!

"Ow!" Renee cried as a hidden board flipped up and hit her in the back. The blow sent her flying forward. Stumbling. Falling. Into the pit beneath the gangplank!

Flailing, she grabbed onto the edge of the overhang and clung to it for dear life.

"Help!" Renee screamed.

"Hang on!" Paul called. Immediately he plowed ahead into the obstacle course.

Light and quick, he managed to dodge the first swinging blade and leap easily over the second. He reached Renee in a flash.

"Take my hand," he said, bending down to pull her out of the pit. It was a struggle, but Paul was able to get her up.

"Are you all right?" Shannon called, her voice pinched with fear.

It took a minute for Renee to answer. She had
to stand up first and regain her footing. Her voice
still shook a little when she answered.

"Yes. I am now."

George let out a long sigh of relief.

"Can you reach the rope, Paul?" Shannon called.

"No, let me," Renee said, quickly reaching up
to grab it.

She had to lean forward, slightly over the pit, to
grab the rope that dangled over her head. *If she
leans much more,* George thought, *she'll fall into the
pit again.* But if she caught the rope, it wouldn't
matter. She could swing on it to the other side. It
was the only way to reach the skeleton.

"You're almost there!" George called. He realized that he'd been holding his breath.

Renee stretched out on her tiptoes and leaned
a little more. Her weight fell forward.

"Got it," she started to call as her hand closed
around the rope, but then it gave way.

Broken!

George's eyes darted up to the ceiling. He
could see now that the rope was frayed where it
connected to a hook on the ceiling.

It was another booby trap, and Renee was
falling into nothingness. *"Ahhh!"* she cried, tum-
bling forward.

Paul lunged out to catch her. She grabbed his arms, pulling him down. His body hurtled toward the pit, too. But at the last instant they both grabbed onto the gangplank.

"I can't hold on!" he called. "I'm slipping!"

Without a moment's thought, George rushed forward. He bolted into the chamber. Ducked under the first cutlass. Scissor-legged over the second one. And dove toward the gangplank.

"Take my hand!" George called to Renee, who was dangling in the pit.

As she grabbed his hand, she almost pulled George down with her. Desperately he lunged backward. With another lunge he was able to drag her out. At the same time, he grabbed Paul's arm and hoisted him up, too.

"Oh, wow, you saved my life," Renee said, shaking.

"Mine too," Paul said, in shock.

"Way to go, George!" Derrick shouted from the cave behind.

George's heart was hammering in his chest. Suddenly it was like all the fear caught up with him, hitting him in the face.

What if he'd been swiped in the neck by that sharp blade? What if he'd fallen into the pit, too?

"I don't believe I just did that," George said, laughing to let off some of the delayed panic.

"Why *did* you?" Paul asked. "No one down here would have done that for me. You don't even know me, but you saved my life."

George didn't know what to say. He could feel himself blushing. "I dunno, Paul," he mumbled. "I just did it without thinking."

Paul's eyes were wide. He kept staring at George.

"Come back," Derrick called, "before you all three fall in that hole again and *I* have to save you."

"Is that a threat?" George joked.

"Yeah. That's my point," Derrick agreed.

"Not till we get the cat-o'-nine-tails," George answered, shaking his head firmly. He glanced around the chamber and spotted the board that had hit Renee in the back. "Do you think we can stretch that thing across the pit?" he wondered.

There was only one way to find out. Renee and Paul hoisted the plank up and rested one end of it on the gangplank. They let the other end fall forward.

It made a bridge across the deep pit, just barely reaching the other side.

"Yes!" Renee cheered. "I'll go," she offered. "I'm great at the balance beam."

"No way," George said, holding her back. "You've been through enough. I'm going." He stepped up onto the gangplank carefully. The loose board—the one forming the temporary bridge—wobbled under his weight. It sent a shiver down his spine.

Don't look down, he told himself. *Just walk across, get the treasure, and walk back.*

He held his breath and tried not to look into the pit. Instead he gazed into the skeleton's empty eye sockets until he was standing next to him.

Whoever you are, I sure hope you can make this trip worthwhile, George thought as he grabbed the cat-o'-nine-tails from the bony grasp.

Twelve

Promises Broken

"Is the diamond in it? In the handle?" Shannon called.

George didn't answer until he was safely back away from the obstacle course, on solid ground. He barely had a chance to catch his breath.

"I don't know," he said. He studied the handle of the cat-o'-nine-tails. A wooden plug in the end looked like it should come off, but he couldn't get it to budge.

"What diamond?" Paul asked.

Oh, man, George thought. Now they were going to have to explain what a diamond was.

"It's a . . . a stone . . ." George started.

"I *know* what it is," Paul snapped. "I've just never seen one."

Oh. Right.

Ooomph! George pulled with all his might, and finally the plug came off.

He shone his helmet light inside.

"It's the map!" he said, half disappointed, half thrilled.

"Pull it out," Derrick said.

George put his fingers inside the hollow handle of the whip. He tried to grasp the paper rolled up inside. But it was stuck, and it felt brittle. He didn't want to crumble it getting it out.

Two scrawny cats ran past him, hissing and chasing a rat. George jumped back and stepped in something gushy. *Oh, no. I'm not even going to look at what that was.*

Yuck. This place was really getting to him! And the stench was getting hard to take.

"We should do this at home," he said, checking his watch. "I have to get back soon, anyway. I need to wash up before my dad and I go to my grand-mother's."

"Oh, come on!" Shannon complained. "We just found another treasure map! We've got to at least *look* at it."

George shook his head. "This map is really *old*, guys. It could crumble to dust if we aren't careful."

Reluctantly his friends nodded. They knew he was right.

"Okay, we'll meet tomorrow at my house," Renee said. She turned to Paul and asked gently, "Can you come?"

"To the dayside?" He shook his head hard. "No."

That's weird, George thought. Paul wasn't afraid

of rats or the dark or being alone. Or even of Leroy's men. But he seemed afraid to come up to the daylight world aboveground.

"Okay," Renee said with a shrug. "Well, we'll look at the map and then show you next time."

"What about the Oreos?" Paul said.

"Oh! I'll bring those next time, too," Shannon said.

"No," Paul said. "Now."

"*Now?* But I can't," Shannon said. "I have to be home soon."

"Why?" Paul asked, looking completely puzzled.

"Why? Because my parents . . ." Shannon's voice trailed off. George knew what she was thinking: How could she explain it to him? Paul didn't understand a lot of things about the way they lived on the dayside.

"You *promised*," Paul interrupted her. "Two bags of Oreos. I want them now."

He crossed his arms and just stood there—like he wasn't going to lead them out of the catacombs if she didn't keep her word.

Shannon sighed. "Listen, I really *can't* do it now. But first thing tomorrow morning, I promise. I'll meet you down here. Somewhere. If I can get down . . ."

She glanced at George with a question in her

eyes. George would still be in Connecticut the next morning, and he doubted Renee and Derrick could make it. Going underground alone would violate their pyrate's oath. But Shannon *had* promised Paul . . . and he'd done a lot for them today.

George checked out the worried expressions on his friends' faces. No one seemed to think this was a very good idea. Going underground—alone? With all the dangerous stuff that had happened to them?

It *didn't* seem safe.

But a promise was a promise.

"I'll give you the key to my house," George said finally. "My dad and I are staying overnight in Connecticut, so we'll be gone. You can slip into my basement and use the secret door in the morning."

"Where do you want to meet?" Shannon asked Paul. "Somewhere not too far into the tunnels. Maybe right under your basement, George?"

George looked at Shannon. "Sure," he said. "Just—"

"No, wait," Derrick interrupted. "I don't want to make it hard for you, Shannon, but what if someone follows Paul to the shaftway? Like one of Leroy's men? I think we want to keep that entrance as secret as possible."

Paul shrugged. "Meet me by the old subway station, then."

Shannon seemed to consider this. "All right. That's not too far. And I know how to get there by myself."

Paul nodded. It was settled, then. Shannon would bring the cookies in the morning. Then she'd meet George and Derrick at Renee's house in the afternoon.

"Okay," said Paul. "But whatever you do, don't use your brights."

"Why not?" Shannon said.

"Leroy's men might come back to the subway," Paul said. "If they do, the brights will give you away."

"Oh," said Shannon. "Well, then, I won't use them."

"And no one looks at the map until tomorrow," Derrick said. "Right?"

"Right," George said.

"Right," Shannon and Renee echoed.

Once they were all safely back in George's basement, George had to confront the ugly reality that he was filthy with quicksand and his father was still home. How would he slip by him and clean up? This was going to be a challenge.

"Bye, guys," George called as he helped his friends back out the basement window.

"See you tomorrow at Renee's," Shannon replied.

"Right, Shannon?" George squinted at her up in the bright sunlight. "Be careful down there."

"Oh, I will."

When his friends had gotten to their feet and scrambled off, George looked around. They'd already helped him move all the boxes back in front of the trapdoor. Now he just had to get by his father. He crept to the top of the stairs and listened: nothing. As quietly as he could, he opened the door.

The house was completely silent. George craned his neck in either direction but didn't see his dad. *He must still be up in his study,* George thought. Or maybe he was just hoping. Taking a deep breath, George ran from the basement door, down the hall, and up the stairs. It was hard to tiptoe and run at the same time, but George tried his best. At the top of the stairs he stopped to catch his breath.

So far, so good.

"George?"

Uh-oh. His father's voice was coming from his bedroom. George turned around to see his father standing in the doorway, pulling on a sweater.

"What on earth happened to you?"

George looked down at himself, hoping that he might miraculously look better than he thought, but no. He looked worse, actually. Covered with sticky sand up to his shoulders, his arms and pant legs smeared with soot and grime. This was going to be hard to explain.

"Well, um, Derrick and I—"

"I thought you were going to play video games."
Peter van Gelder was beginning to develop a worried crease between his eyebrows. It made George
nervous. His dad didn't look angry so much as . . .
concerned.

"We did," George said quickly. "But then we got
bored. Derrick said we should . . . um . . . go play
football in the park. And we were in this really
muddy meadow. And I guess we were playing kind
of rough."

George's father frowned and stepped forward,
reaching out to touch George's eyebrow. "What's
this?" he asked, and George winced. He must
have gotten a bruise there when he went through
the trapdoor. He hadn't noticed till now.

"Well, Derrick tackled me, and I fell on a rock.
And it hit my eyebrow."

It was the best George could come up with on the
spot, but he could see that his dad wasn't buying it.

"I didn't know you liked to play football," Peter
van Gelder said.

George shrugged. "It's not my favorite thing,
but it's . . . um . . . not bad."

George's dad just looked at him for a moment.
The crease between his brows remained, but there
was something more—kind of a question in his

eyes. He could tell that his dad thought there was more to the story, if that was the real story at all. And he could tell that it was worrying him.

George just didn't know what else to say.

"Well, hurry into the shower, George," his father said finally, turning away. "We need to catch the six o'clock train. That means we need to get moving."

"Okay, Dad." George scurried to his room and closed the door. He walked over to his mirror and studied his face. *Ouch!* The bruise on his left eyebrow was worse than he'd thought. He could see why his father had looked so concerned.

George put down his backpack, which contained the whip, the pirate flag, and the old coat. He hated lying to his dad like this. But what choice did he have?

"Can I get you some more brussels sprouts, George?"

George looked up from his plate where he was pushing his broiled flounder around. No matter how many times he mentioned to his grandmother that he didn't like seafood, that always seemed to be what she served when he came over for dinner. Not that he held it against her. His mother's mother was a small, old-fashioned, eager-to-please woman, who was getting more and more hard of hearing as the years went on. George wondered whether every time he told her he didn't like seafood, she thought he was saying he *really loved* seafood.

"Um, no thanks, Nana." George was having trouble choking down even the first round. But with his dad sitting right next to him, George knew he had to eat enough to be polite. And he didn't want to make Nana feel bad. She was a sweet lady and the closest relative that remained to his mother.

"How is school, George?" she asked, returning to her meal.

"It's not bad," he told her. "We're studying cell division."

"Television?" His grandmother looked shocked. "Goodness. How things have changed since I was a girl. You watch so much of it, and then you study it in school, too?"

George sighed and poked at his fish. "I mean, we're working on cell division in science class."

"Oh," his grandmother said. But she still looked confused. George got the feeling that she hadn't really heard him.

"What George really enjoys," his father jumped in, speaking loudly, "is history. The other night George and his friends were asking about my studies. And, of course, you know George is very interested in pirates."

"Ah, pirates." George's grandmother smiled. Before George's parents had gotten married and Nana had moved out of the family house, she had been very proud of the history of their house on Windsor Lane. "How fitting since you do have a family connection, George!"

George took a sip of milk and nodded, raising his voice. "Yeah, Captain Kidd. I've been trying to learn more about him."

George's grandmother winked. "They had quite a remarkable romance, you know, Captain Kidd and Sarah Oort. In all of her correspondence with her family, you can see that she was very much in love."

"It's a shame he died so young," George's father said. "They really weren't married that long before he was hanged."

"I would do anything to protect my sweet Sarah, to keep her from heartache," George thought. Captain Kidd's journal showed how much he cared about her. He wondered what it must have been like for him, being hanged so far from his wife and knowing how his death would hurt her. Or what it must have been like for her to learn he was dead.

"But she remarried," George spoke up. "She married Ulysses Pyle and started our family. So she must have fallen in love again."

George's grandmother nodded. "The human heart

is hard to figure out, I suppose. She healed and was married again within a few years. I guess that was common in that time." She sighed, her look far away. "It's odd, though. When I was younger, I worked on constructing our family tree. And I couldn't find much information about Ulysses Pyle."

"Oh, no?" George's father popped a brussels sprout in his mouth. "Well, that's not unusual. As I've told George, they didn't keep very careful records in those days."

"I suppose." George's grandmother frowned. "I mean, I tracked down their marriage license, of course, and the birth announcements of their children. But I couldn't find any information on him before their marriage."

Peter van Gelder looked puzzled. "Perhaps he just led a very ordinary life. Worked at the mill, spent time with his family."

Nana shrugged. "True. It's likely that he was born in another country or that his records were destroyed somehow—fires, floods, you know."

George took one final bite of fish. *Yuck.* He liked visiting Nana, but this seafood problem was getting ridiculous. Still, Nana was a great source of his mother's family history. He wondered now just who Ulysses Pyle had been. But his excitement over the possibilities was kept in check by what he knew Ulysses Pyle was *not*. He was *not* Captain Kidd. And much as he didn't like to admit it, that had always bothered George. It was a little disappointing that, while he lived in Captain Kidd's house and was descended from his true love, George didn't really have any of the privateer's blood in him.

But then when George really thought about it, maybe that was *good*. The things he was learning about Kidd now didn't exactly make him a great guy. Obviously he had something to hide since he'd put so much time and energy into building the underground world. And he'd used *corpses* as part of his treasure hunt. Yuck.

"So," said Nana, putting down her fork and standing up from the table, "who's ready for dessert?"

At two-thirty the next afternoon George and his dad got back to the city. George was a little tired. He hadn't gotten much sleep the night before. When he stayed at Nana's, he had to share the fold-out couch with his father. And Peter van Gelder snored like a tuba all night.

George made a quick grilled cheese sandwich and downed a glass of chocolate milk. Thank goodness for normal food! Then he picked up his backpack, still with the cat-o'-nine-tails inside, and headed for the door. He could barely wait to meet with his friends and check out their latest discovery.

He yanked open the front door and gasped.

"George! Hello! You're just the person I wanted to see!" Mrs. St. John said.

His next-door neighbors, Mr. and Mrs. St. John, were standing right there, blocking his exit.

"Um, hi! I was just going out," George said, hoping they'd move to let him slip past them.

But instead they both moved forward, forcing him to back up into the house so they could come in.

"So George, I understand that you recently had a birthday. Eleven years old!" Mr. St. John said.

George nodded, still hoping to make a quick exit. "That's right."

"I'm sorry we had to miss your party," Mrs. St. John said, brushing her long brown hair out of her face. "But I wanted you to know, George, that we haven't forgotten you." She reached into her tote bag and pulled out a square package wrapped in paper with boats on it, covered with ribbon and bows. She handed it to George. "I bought this a few months ago, and I've been saving it for your birthday. From all of our conversations, I thought it might be something you'd enjoy." Mrs. St. John looked down at George with a shy, hopeful smile.

George took the package—whoa, it was heavy!—
and smiled back.

He looked down at the extravagantly wrapped
gift. Well, it looked like he would be delayed for a
bit. But there was nothing wrong with an extra
birthday present. "Wow, thanks." He lifted it up
and pretended to shake it, which was difficult
because the package was so heavy. What kind of
present would the St. Johns give him? They owned
a small electronics store—that probably meant a
CD player? A video game? "Can I open it now?"
he asked.

Mr. St. John chuckled. "Certainly, George. We
wouldn't dream of making you wait."

Leaning against the door frame, George tackled
the package, ripping off the ribbons and bows.
Mrs. St. John sure did like to use tape! When he
finally got the wrapping off, he was faced with even
more wrapping—this time bubble wrap. George
carefully slipped his finger under the tape and
peeled it off. The bubble wrap parted to reveal . . .
a book. A really old book, by the looks of it.

"Um . . . thanks!" George said, not sure how to
react. "It's . . . um . . ."

"Do you know what it is?" Mr. St. John asked,
his eyes dancing.

"Well . . ." George ran his hand over the dusty

marbled green cover. There was no title on the front. "No. Not really."

Mrs. St. John leaned forward eagerly. "Look at the title!" she urged excitedly. She took the book from George's hand and flipped open the front cover. She pointed to the title page with one carefully manicured pink finger. "See, George? It's very, very old."

George looked down where her finger was pointing and read the title. *The History of the Pirates, Freebooters, or Buccaneers of America,* by J. M. von Archenholtz. "Wow!"

"It was printed in London in 1807," Mrs. St. John rushed on. "It's very rare, an antique. I thought . . ." She shot George a nervous glance and smiled. "I know you're very interested in pirates, George, because of your special connection to Captain Kidd. I saw this at a used bookstore recently, and I thought you might enjoy reading what people thought about your pirates hundreds of years ago. I hope you like it."

"Oh, I do, I definitely do!" George began to gently flip through the pages, and phrases leaped out at him from the brown and age-softened paper. *Heartless scourges . . . killing without conscience . . . hoarders of treasure!* This book looked really cool! The books his dad had given him were all written recently. It would be great to look back and see what people thought about pirates way back in the early 1800s.

"I'm so glad!" Mrs. St. John gave him a million-watt smile. Behind her, Mr. St. John reached over to pat him on the shoulder.

"Happy birthday, George."

"Thank you so much." George reached over to give Mrs. St. John a hug. She patted his back affectionately.

"You're getting so big, George. Before we know it, you'll be off to high school and then applying to colleges! And then who will tell me about pirates?"

George leaned back, and if he wasn't mistaken, Mrs. St. John reached up and quickly wiped a tear from the corner of her eye. He looked at Mr. St. John, who winked at him. *The St. Johns are so nice to me,* George thought. *Mrs. St. John is one of the only people who'll listen to me rattle on about pirates as long as I want. They'd be great parents. I wonder why they don't have kids?*

"Well, I'll be here for at least seven more years, Mrs. St. John," George said. "So I'll have to read through this whole book and come up with lots of conversation topics."

Mrs. St. John laughed. "All right, then." She

gave George another hug, then smiled. "Is your father home, George?"

"Yeah," said George, "he's in the kitchen." He placed the book at the bottom of the stairs, where he'd remember to bring it up to his room.

"Well . . ." Mrs. St. John looked back at her husband. "We should go find him. Have a good afternoon, George."

"You too," George replied, stepping onto the sidewalk. "And thanks again."

"You're very welcome."

Mr. St. John stepped inside, and Mrs. St. John followed him, removing her coat. Suddenly George was transfixed.

Wait a minute!

Underneath her coat Mrs. St. John was wearing a simple black turtleneck. But as she turned to enter the kitchen, something about her profile struck a chord with George. She looked strangely, suddenly very familiar—but not just because she was his next-door neighbor. It was something more recent than that, something—

Oh, man!

She looked just like the woman from the tunnels!

Mrs. St. John looked back at him, and George realized he was standing there staring with his mouth open. Still struggling to figure it out, he forced himself to wave and head off down the street. But as he walked, a million thoughts were flying through his head. *Why would Mrs. St. John be down in the tunnels?* He went over and over the question but couldn't find an acceptable answer. Did she have one of the maps? No. Had she ever seen the journal? No. Did she even know anything about Litaria or the Eye of Eternity? No.

He shook his head, trying to make sense of it all. Well, there was only one rational explanation.

He was wrong. If he'd seen anyone in the tunnels at all, it couldn't have been Mrs. St. John.

He hurried to Renee's.

"I'm early," he announced when she opened her apartment door. "But I couldn't wait any longer."

"No problem," she said. "I'll call Derrick and Shannon and see if they can come early, too."

"I already called Derrick," George said. "He's on his way."

Renee nodded and picked up a cordless phone.

Dialing, she grabbed George's wrist, pulled him into her room, and closed the door.

"Hello, Mrs. Starling? This is Renee. May I speak to Shannon?" Renee asked.

George watched as Renee's face turned stark white and serious.

She closed her eyes and covered her mouth with her hand.

"Oh, uh, yeah," Renee said quickly. "She did. She was here. But she left just a few minutes ago. I thought she was going home, but maybe she's going to George's house. I'll call her there. Thanks!"

Then she said good-bye and hung up.

"What happened?" George asked.

"Shannon left her house early this morning and hasn't been back since!" Renee said. "She told her mother she was going to my house. I had to cover for her."

"Oh, no," George said. "How early?"

"Like at nine o'clock," Renee said.

George checked the time. It was almost four. Shannon had been gone seven hours. No *way* would it take that long to deliver the cookies to Paul.

"Whoa," he said softly. He flopped down on the green-and-pink quilt on Renee's bed. "Do you think something happened?"

"Maybe she got lost underground on her way to meet Paul," Renee said.

"Not likely," George said. "We all know the way to the subway station by now."

"Yeah, but what if she had to hide from someone? One of Leroy's men?" Renee said.

George shuddered. He hated thinking about Shannon facing Leroy's thugs alone. Why had he let her go down?

"I hope she didn't fall," Renee mumbled.

"Even if she did, she'd come back," George said.

"Even if she was hurt?" Renee wondered.

George swallowed hard. This was what he had been afraid of. That something terrible would happen to one of his friends.

Renee's door buzzer rang. George and Renee both leaped up.

"I'll get it!" she called to her mom as she raced to the front door.

Please let it be Shannon, George thought. *Please!*

But when they opened the door, it was only Derrick standing there.

"Shannon's missing," George explained quickly.

"Missing?" Derrick said. "How?"

"I don't know," George said. "But we've got to go down to the tunnels and find her—right now!"

Thirteen

The Trail

"Shhh!" George put a finger to his mouth.

He, Renee, and Derrick had slipped in through his basement window.

As quietly as they could, they were putting on their gear.

George could hear his father's voice upstairs.

He's talking to the St. Johns, George realized.

"Quiet," George whispered very softly. "He'll hear us."

Moving slowly so he wouldn't make any noise, George ducked into the hole under the chimney. He lifted the octagonal handle on the secret door.

Down. First George. Then Derrick. Then Renee.

They were getting so good at this rope business, George didn't even get a funny upside-down feeling in his stomach anymore. In fact, *this* part was fun. But when he touched down in the tunnel, the bad feeling returned.

Knowing that Shannon was lost down there

made the place seem dangerous all over again.

"Keep your eyes peeled for signs," Renee said as they walked along the streambed.

"Like what?" Derrick asked.

"Signs of a struggle," Renee said.

Yikes. George's heart picked up speed again. He didn't want to think about that: Shannon fighting with Leroy's men.

That would be awful. There was no *way* she could win.

Without even discussing it, they headed straight for the old abandoned subway station. It seemed like the best place to find Paul—who could hopefully tell them where Shannon was.

Sure enough, Paul was lying on a cardboard box in what remained of the shantytown on the old tracks. The former residents had cleaned the place out, and now only a couple of boxes and old pieces of clothing remained.

"Hey," George called, shining his light sideways to avoid hurting Paul's eyes.

Paul sat up and frowned at them.

"Did you bring them?" he asked. "The Oreos?"

"No," George said. "Didn't Shannon?"

"She promised, but she never showed," Paul complained. "I waited here all morning."

"Are you sure?" George asked.

Suddenly it occurred to him: What if Shannon had come, but Paul hadn't been there?

"How do you know when it's morning?" George asked.

"When the sun comes up," Paul said, "I can see the light coming in some places."

George nodded. *Okay. But the sun comes up at six-thirty or something.* Shannon wouldn't have been there till nine-thirty or ten. Maybe by the time she'd shown up, Paul had been gone.

There was no way to know. They'd just have to hunt for her.

"Let's spread out," George said to Renee and Derrick.

"Bad plan," Derrick said. "We'll *all* get lost."

"No, we won't," Renee said. "I brought the walkie-talkies this time."

"Why? They don't work down here," Derrick said.

"Sometimes they do," Renee said. "If you're in the right spot. Anyway, they're better than nothing."

"Right," George said. "And just in case they don't work, we'll have a backup plan. Meet back here in thirty minutes if we haven't found Shannon."

His friends all nodded and checked their watches.

"I'll help," Paul offered.

"Okay," Derrick said. "You can come with me."

The four of them spread out. Renee headed

back down toward the streambed. Another tunnel was down there—one that *wasn't* on their maps. Maybe Shannon had taken a wrong turn.

Derrick and Paul went north, down the old subway tracks. Past the shantytown.

And George decided to go south along the tracks, the way they'd gone the other day. Toward the door with Leroy's name on it. The spider closet.

George held his helmet light in his hands, aiming it up, down, and sideways. Checking out the tunnel, he squinted as he looked up the track.

How far did this thing go, anyway? All the way downtown?

Or was it what they called a "spur"—a small track off to the side, where the trains could go to get out of the way when they weren't running?

He couldn't tell yet, but . . .

"Whoa!" George blurted out as his light hit something on the ground.

He stopped, frozen. Was that what he thought it was?

He bent down to pick it up.

It was a small blue piece of shiny paper. New. And clean.

It was the corner from a bag of Oreos!

His heart jumped into high gear. This time it felt like it was pounding in his throat.

Back and forth he swung his helmet light, scanning the ground, searching for more.

Oh, man, George thought. There was another piece of blue packaging.

And beyond that a piece of an Oreo cookie!

He grabbed his walkie-talkie and pressed the talk button as fast as he could.

"Renee? Derrick? Come in. I've found something!"

Hsssss. Nothing came back. Nothing except the static hissing sound that meant the walkie-talkies weren't working.

"Hello? Derrick! Come in!" he repeated, pressing his mouth tightly to the walkie-talkie.

Hssssss. Nothing!

George stuffed the walkie-talkie in his pocket and took a few small steps forward. He scanned the ground again with his light. There was another broken piece of cookie a few steps down the track. And then another. It looked for all the world like Shannon had left a trail of cookie crumbs. Just like Hansel and Gretel.

George followed the trail for another twenty or thirty feet. Past the spider closet.

Suddenly his walkie-talkie sprang to life.

"George?" he heard a crackling voice say.

He yanked it out of his pocket and pressed talk.

"Derrick? I think I found something! Over."

"What?" Derrick's voice came back, but it was hard to hear. There was a lot of static. "Did you find Shannon?"

"I found her trail! Can you hear me?" George said.

"What? Repeat that," Derrick said. "Where are you?"

"I'm on the south part of the old subway track!" George said. "Come find me!"

Hssssss. A lot of crackling and static.

"Derrick? Are you there?" George called.

Nothing.

"Can you hear me, Derrick? Come in," George said.

Nothing.

Jeez.

George walked on about forty feet more, his light aimed downward, following the cookie trail.

Where was it leading?

A knot began to form in his stomach. The trail of cookies on the ground could mean only one thing: Shannon was in trouble. She was trying to tell them something—trying to leave them a clue.

Otherwise she wouldn't be wasting good Oreos like that!

George forced himself to put one foot in front of the other while wild scenarios ran through his head. It was clear that something terrible had happened—that Leroy's men had probably found Shannon. What would they do to her?

He pictured her tied to a chair in a dark room, bright lights trained on her eyes as she was interrogated. Or maybe Leroy's men had already decided she was expendable and had tied her to some *working* subway tracks and were watching, waiting for her to be smushed.

George pushed that image from his mind and concentrated on the trail.

Another piece of Oreo. Here the tunnel turned slightly. To the left.

All of a sudden the cookie trail came to a stop.

How come? George wondered. *Did she run out? Was she forced to stop?*

He shone his light left, then right. Then straight ahead on the tracks.

Wait—the tracks ended here. In fact, so did the tunnel.

A few hundred feet ahead of him was a solid stone wall.

So the tunnel was for a spur, not a main track, George realized. *Wait a minute,* he thought. This didn't make sense. Why would Leroy's thugs drag Shannon down to a dead end?

This tunnel must lead somewhere, George thought. *There must be a way out of here.*

He shone his light to the left. *Wait—back there!* Very slowly George shifted his light back over the wall. It was small, easy enough to miss in the dark, but sure enough—there was a nook. All kinds of old lengths of lumber were leaning up against the wall, in the corner. It looked like maybe, a long time ago, there was some kind of train storage area back here.

George crept over to the lumber and shined his light behind it.

Bingo! There was a door.

The lumber camouflaged it well. But without even moving the boards, George could slip behind them and in through a door that opened into . . .

Where *was* he?

It looked like some kind of basement or storage room. It was pitch-black, but his helmet light revealed a small room cluttered with cleaning supplies. Push brooms. A bucket. A mop. Some other rusty old things that George couldn't identify. But the room was relatively neat, free of cobwebs and dirt. There was a clear path from the doorway to another door. George crept through it and found himself standing in a full-sized basement. It seemed to be the lower part of an old warehouse.

This feels wrong, George thought. *Like I'm walking into a trap. This is too easy.* He felt like at any instant, he would turn a corner and find Shannon tied to a chair or something. And Leroy's thugs surrounding her, ready to shove him into a big sack.

But he was certain Shannon had been here. And right now, exploring this space was the only hope he had of finding her. He tiptoed softly through the basement.

He turned a corner and froze.

"Whoa," George said softly.

There was an elevator right in front of him, its door standing open like an invitation. Above the elevator was a light-up sign with only two floors: "B" and "5." "B" was lit up. George stood stock-still, unsure what to do. His heart hammered so hard now, he felt like he couldn't breathe. But he forced himself to step inside and look at the buttons.

There was only one. Up.

Well, George thought, *the trail leads here. What should I do?*

He had no idea where Renee, Derrick, and Paul were or whether he should try to find them before going up in the elevator alone. But the more he thought about it, the more urgent it felt that he go up there—now. Shannon had already been gone for *seven* hours. Who knew what might happen to her in the minutes he waited for his friends to catch up?

Well, this is it, he thought. *I can't stop now if I'm going to find Shannon.*

He took off his helmet and stuffed it into his backpack. Then he reached out toward the panel and pushed the button.

Fourteen

Fast Talk

The elevator rose slowly and then stopped with a bounce. In the moment before the doors opened, George fought the desire to run. To just pound on the elevator button and get out of there while the getting was good.

I'm trespassing, he thought. *And who knows what's going to be on the other side of this door?* If George was right—if this was where Shannon had been taken—then he was walking into the headquarters of some superbad guys.

And possibly walking right into a trap.

Then the elevator door slid open and George peered into . . . what?

It was an apartment. Or a loft—an old warehouse loft—that had been converted into a beautiful new apartment.

Wow, George thought as he stepped into the space. Soft music was playing on the stereo system. Thick Persian rugs covered the polished hardwood floor. A lush black leather sofa was decorated with velvet throw pillows and a tapestry blanket. Colorful paintings and artwork adorned the walls.

Where am I? George wondered. *Who lives here? And how are they connected to Leroy?*

As he stood in the middle of the living room, he heard a voice. Then footsteps. George froze; someone was coming! And there was no time to run—and no place to run to! He could feel his heart thundering in his chest. Whoever it was came down the hall, talking on a cordless phone.

"But the Litarian prime minister will have to . . ." a man's voice was saying as a tall figure walked into the living room.

George's mouth dropped open.

It was his neighbor, Mr. Roulain!

Oh, man, George thought, his head swimming with questions and pounding with fear.

Mr. Roulain isn't mixed up in this thing with Leroy—is he?

No way. He couldn't be. Roulain was such a cool guy—not just hipper than most adults, but nicer, more relaxed. Even now he was wearing a Bruce Springsteen T-shirt and faded blue jeans. He looked like a teenager, not like one of Leroy's thugs.

But if he's not looking for the diamond, why was he just talking on the phone about Litaria? And why did the trail lead here, to his apartment?

Suddenly Roulain stopped and froze, midsentence. He stared at George in surprise. "Uh, I'll have to call you back," he said into the phone. Then he clicked off.

He looked at George in pure confusion. George struggled to think of something to say.

"Uh, hi," George said finally. He could hear his voice cracking with nervousness. He glanced down at his clothes and the climbing gear he was wearing. His harness was still attached to his waist and legs. Carabiners dangled from his belt.

How was he going to explain all *this*?

"Uh, I can't believe I just walked into your apartment," George mumbled, talking fast. "I'm really sorry. I was just, uh, doing a project for school about underground waterways in New York City, and I found these tunnels and I sort of got lost and . . ."

Mr. Roulain was still staring at him, gripping the cordless phone. His eyes were steely. Like he didn't believe a word George was saying.

"So anyway, while I was trying to find my way out, I came to this building and saw this elevator," George went on, superfast. "So I just sort of got in it and pushed the button and guess what? It opened right here, in your house. I'm sorry—honestly. I didn't mean to barge in."

Roulain stared for a moment more. Then he nodded and gave George a tight smile.

"All right, George," he said. "Don't panic. It was an honest mistake, I can see that."

Phew! George thought. But for some reason, he still didn't really feel like Mr. Roulain believed him.

"I'd love to have you stay and visit," Mr. Roulain went on. "But I was just on my way out. Maybe you'll come another time?"

"Sure," George said.

Roulain began walking toward the door, then turned back, like he was expecting George to follow.

What do I do now? George wondered. He still didn't know where Shannon was. All the clues led up here. Had she been able to sneak out?

"Perhaps you'd like to take the stairs and the front door this time," Roulain joked. "It's much easier."

"Yeah," George said with an embarrassed laugh.

It looked like he was going to have to leave to avoid any more awkwardness with Mr. Roulain. George glanced around one more time just in case. Was anything important here? A clue?

It didn't look that way. This was just a nice, big loft apartment with a kitchen that opened into the huge main room. A coat closet by the front door. And two other doors, closed. One probably led to the bedroom. The other . . . who knew?

George started to follow Mr. Roulain out the front door. All of a sudden, out of the corner of his eye, he saw something. On the floor.

His head snapped back toward the closed door on the left.

What was that, lying on the carpet just outside the door?

George's heart jumped right up into his throat.

It was a blue piece of plastic. From a package of Oreos!

"Shannon!" George blurted without thinking.

"Mmmmph!" George heard from behind the door. That was Shannon's voice!

Fifteen

Kidnapped

George's head snapped to Mr. Roulain.

Yikes! He is *working for Leroy! And they've got Shannon!*

George started to bolt, he wasn't sure where. But Mr. Roulain was fast and strong. In two quick steps he darted to block George's escape. His huge, muscular arms wrapped around George's shoulders, shoving him toward the room where Shannon was.

"I don't know how much you know," Mr. Roulain growled as he lifted George, "but for your sake, I hope it isn't much."

"Let me go!" George cried, struggling to get away. He tried to kick Mr. Roulain in the shins but missed. Mr. Roulain squeezed tighter. Forcefully he wrestled George aside so he could work the key in the door lock. The door swung open with a *thunk*. Inside, George could see Shannon sitting on a washing machine. It must be the laundry room. Someone had tied a necktie around her mouth, and her hands were tied together behind her back.

"*Eoooorrrjje!*" Shannon cried as Mr. Roulain shoved George into the room.

"Now I've got *two* of you to deal with," Mr. Roulain mumbled, angrily shaking his head. "You should have stayed home, George."

His voice was cold and his gaze hard. He reached into the dryer and pulled out a white sock, then roughly swung it over George's head and into his mouth. He yanked the ends and tied it tightly behind George's head.

"*Owww!*" George whined.

"Quiet." Mr. Roulain pulled another sock out of the dryer, then wrestled George's hands behind his back and quickly tied them. George couldn't believe it. How could this be his kindly neighbor? How long would he be in here?

"You're messing with things that are way over your head," Mr. Roulain said, then looked at George and Shannon and sighed. "You two behave now. Don't make any noise." Then he walked out the door, closing it behind him and locking it.

Shannon and George looked at each other. Shannon's face was pale. Her red-and-orange-dyed hair was a mess. And her clothes were wrinkled. She looked like she'd put up quite a fight.

George began to wiggle his hands behind his

back, and soon he'd loosened the sock's hold. Mr. Roulain had been in a hurry when he'd tied it. Apparently he hadn't done a very good job.

"Mmmmph!" cried Shannon.

George nodded and pulled hard. He'd managed to get his hands free! Quickly he yanked the gag off his mouth. "Are you okay?" he whispered, grabbing Shannon's gag and pulling it down.

Shannon let out a huge sigh of relief. "I think so," she whispered after a minute. She turned to the side so George could reach her tied hands. In seconds he undid the knot, and she shook her hands free.

"This is unbelievable." George moaned softly. "What happened?"

Shannon frowned, looking upset with herself. "It was my fault," she whispered, shaking her head. "I went against Paul's advice. I brought a flashlight with me just in case, and I figured I'd turn it off when I got near the subway station. But when I got there, my eyes were so used to the light, I couldn't make out *anything*. I thought I would flick on the flashlight just for a minute to see where I was. But as soon as I did . . ."

Oh, man. George waited for her to explain, but Shannon suddenly sat up and put a finger to her lips.

She went to the door to listen. They could hear Roulain moving around out there, doing something.

Then they heard the front door open and close. They sat still for a minute, but they couldn't hear Roulain in the apartment anymore. When they were sure he was gone, they both relaxed a bit. George quickly checked out their surroundings.

The laundry room was nearly empty except for the washer and dryer. Two crude wooden shelves held a big bottle of detergent and a box of fabric softener sheets. There was a set of drying racks, also empty, an ironing board, and an iron.

Then he noticed the window.

"Can we get out this way?" he asked, hurrying to look.

Shannon shook her head. "I already checked. We're too high up. We'd break our necks if we tried to jump. There's no fire escape. And no one will hear us if we yell."

George gazed down. They were at least five stories up. And the window looked out across a deserted alley on a brick wall. No one would see them even if they waved their arms.

We're trapped, he thought miserably. *Totally trapped.*

"So what happened?" he asked Shannon.

Shannon sighed. "Leroy's men were a few yards down the tracks—digging away like crazy. They had all kinds of fancy equipment, too. I mean, serious stuff."

"Like what?" George asked.

"I don't know—all kinds of electronic gadgets," Shannon said. "Meters and listening devices and cameras. It looked like high-tech spy stuff."

"Wow," George said. "I thought they were just a bunch of thugs."

"They're well-equipped thugs, if you ask me," Shannon said. "Anyway, as soon as I flicked on my light, one of the guys spotted me and grabbed me before I could get away."

"What did he look like?" George asked. "Was it Mr. Roulain?"

"No, no." Shannon shook her head quickly. "It was just a guy in black jeans and a black shirt. And a shaved head. One of Leroy's heavies."

George sighed. "Whoa. This is too much. And now Mr. Roulain's working for Leroy."

Shannon gave him a funny look.

"What?" George demanded.

"No, George," Shannon said. "Mr. Roulain *is* Leroy."

George couldn't believe it. "Seriously?" he asked. George thought about all the times he'd talked to Mr. Roulain. How great he was. How he'd given George this really neat watch for his birthday. How he'd seemed like such a friendly guy.

"Leroy has been bossing people around down there for years," George said. "At least that's what Paul told me."

"So?" Shannon didn't get his point.

"It's just hard to believe that Mr. Roulain has spent so much of his life digging for Captain Kidd's treasure," George said. "Although . . ."

"What?" Shannon asked.

"Come to think of it, my dad's been talking about him forever," George said. "About the fact that he never goes to work in the daytime. He used to work for the electric company, but a few years ago he quit his job. We wondered what he did."

"Well, now you know!" Shannon blurted. "He's got a day job—and a night job. Underground!"

George's head was spinning. He couldn't put all this together and have it make sense.

"I wonder why he calls himself Leroy," George muttered.

"It's French for 'the king,'" Shannon explained. "*Le roi*. I guess he's French."

"The king of what?" George said.

"King of the underground," Shannon said. "That's what the guy who grabbed me and dragged me up here told me."

"Unbelievable," George said. "But this still doesn't add up. Years searching for a diamond? They'd be better off digging in Africa!"

"I'm betting the Eye of Eternity is worth more than a million," Shannon said. "A *lot* more."

George nodded. It had to be.

Shannon shrugged. "Anyway, Roulain said that I know too much," she added with a shiver. "Now he has to figure out what to do with me."

"With *us*," George corrected her.

They both stood there for a minute, staring at each other. George could see fear in Shannon's eyes. He'd never seen that before. Not in her.

"We've got to get out of here," he said. How much time did they have before Roulain came back? There was no way to know.

George glanced around the room, looking for something heavy. Maybe there was something they could use to break down the door.

"Hey—what about this?" he said. "We could tie all of Roulain's blue jeans together to make a rope and—"

He turned back to Shannon and nearly jumped out of his skin.

"*Ahhhhhhhh!*" he screamed.

A face was staring at him through the fifth-story window!

Sixteen

Surprise

"*Ahhh!*" Shannon screamed and jumped when George did. "What's wrong?"

George jerked in surprise, then almost laughed.

"Look!" he said, racing to the window.

It was Renee! She was peering into the window, tapping on the glass.

"Open up!" she said, her voice muffled by the glass.

"Wow!" Shannon yelped happily. She hurried to help George lift the window so Renee could climb in. Renee was all hooked up with a rope and her other climbing gear.

"I don't believe you!" Shannon said, hugging Renee. "Did you *climb* all the way up here? All five stories? You are the *best*!"

Renee smiled and gave a humble shrug. "It wasn't too hard," she said. "Are you guys all right?"

"No! We're being held prisoners in here!" Shannon said.

George shook his head in disbelief. "How did you get up here? What's that rope attached to?"

"Oh." Renee looked back at the rope and grinned. "Well, Derrick and I figured out that you must be in this apartment—I'll explain that later. Anyway, we were looking all over for a way to get up here, and then I found the fire escape on the other side of the building. Derrick jumped up and grabbed the first ladder for me, and I grabbed my equipment and climbed all the way up—straight up to the roof!"

Shannon looked at her friend in amazement. "So how'd you get here?"

"Once I was on the roof, I found the handle to the trapdoor that the tenants use to get up there. It was perfect for connecting this rope to—and then I just hung it over the side of the building where Roulain's apartment was."

George chuckled. "So you're all hooked up and everything?"

Renee nodded and gave her harness a tug. "Safety first, baby."

Shannon leaned her head out the window and followed the rope down with her eyes. "There's Derrick!" She grinned and waved. "Hey, Derrick!"

"Hey!" George heard his best friend's voice echo up from the sidewalk. "Hurry up!"

Shannon leaned back in. "How did you know which window?"

"Derrick helped figure it out." Renee was beginning to unhook herself from her climbing equipment. "We'll explain everything once you're safe."

"Let's get out, then," Shannon said.

Renee was so calm and cool, George was impressed all over again. She hooked up the rope to his harness and showed him how to climb down.

"Just do it like we did in the tunnels underground," Renee explained. "Except remember that there are more windows right below this one. So be careful when you're rappelling. Don't stick your feet through them."

"Windows?" asked George. "Uh-oh. What if someone sees us? How will we explain climbing down the side of the building?"

Renee shrugged. "Well, luckily, we're on the alley side of the building—not right out on the street. But we need to be as quiet as possible and hope no one notices. As long as no one's looking out into the alley, we should be okay."

Renee helped George climb out of the window and get settled on the rope. He looked up at the sky, at the buildings on the next block over—anything to avoid looking down. His hands were all sweaty. *I wonder how hard your heart can pound in your chest before it explodes,* George thought.

There he was, dangling on a rope five stories above the ground. He glanced to the side. A light breeze was blowing. Dust blew into his eyes from Windsor Lane. The streetlights looked pinkish from up here. Two neon lights from a building a few blocks away flashed red in the distance.

Then he glanced down.

Big mistake.

It only made the flip-flopping in his stomach much worse.

This whole thing was ten times scarier than going down in the tunnel underground. For one thing, he could see how far he was going to fall— if the rope let go.

Slowly he let the rope out, little by little, lowering himself.

"Hurry up," Shannon called in a loud whisper from above.

Oh, yeah. He *did* have to hurry! What if Roulain came back while Shannon and Renee were still up there?

George went faster and lost some control. He started swinging. Dangling. Twirling. He kicked wildly, then realized that his feet were just inches away from the window below. Struggling to balance himself, he regained control. He glanced through the window: a kid's bedroom. Brightly colored toys, a bunk bed, and fortunately, no kid. Slowly he continued past some empty offices, closer to Derrick, who was waiting on the sidewalk. Finally he touched down. Back on the ground. Safe and sound.

It took Shannon a lot less time to make the same descent. Then Renee came last.

"Hurry, Renee!" Shannon hissed from the ground. "Roulain could be back any minute!"

Renee nodded and lowered herself some more. Then she stopped and looked at a window she was passing.

George could see that it was open.

Wait a minute, thought George. *None of those windows were open when I went by.*

Just as he had that thought, he heard Renee. "Oh, no!" she called. "Oh, *no!*"

"MMMOMMMMMMMMMM!"

The shriek coming from inside the window was louder than George could have ever imagined. He felt his heart clench. *It's over,* he thought. *There's no way we can explain this.*

"MMMMOOOOOMMMMM! There's someone outside my win-doooow!"

"Hurry, Renee!" Derrick shouted. It was the first time any of them had raised one of their voices since George started rappelling down. Derrick's call seemed to prod Renee into action. She had frozen for a minute, seemingly in shock. "Come on! Get down before his mom can come!"

Renee grabbed the rope and rappelled down the face of the building faster than any of them had done. At the bottom Shannon, George, and Derrick all converged on her, unhitching her from the rope and grabbing equipment as fast as they could.

"Down there!" they heard from the window above. George looked up, and he could see a little blond boy looking down, pointing with a pudgy finger. "She was outside my window!"

"Let's get *out* of here," Renee said. "Before his mom gets a look at us."

Moving as fast as they could, they ran out of the alley to the street and around the corner. George kept running, and the others followed. Finally he came to rest in front of a small park four blocks away. For a moment no one said anything, they were so busy panting and catching their breath.

"What happened to you guys?" Derrick gasped after a few seconds.

They all sat down on a bench while George and Shannon explained what had happened to them. All about Roulain being Leroy. And about the men digging.

George finished the story and looked at Derrick and Renee. "But what I want to know is: how did *you guys* find us?"

"Well," Derrick said, stretching out his legs, "you know Paul and I heard you on the walkie-talkie. So I called Renee, and we went to meet up with you in the old subway tunnel. You were nowhere to be found, but we found this cookie trail."

"Made of Oreos," Renee added.

"So we knew that Shannon must have been there," Derrick continued. "In fact, I thought maybe that was what you were trying to tell me about on the walkie-talkie."

George nodded. "Yup. So you followed the trail?"

Renee picked up the story. "We followed it to the end of the tunnel, and then we found these doors leading to an elevator. And there was a sign on top with a 'B' and a '5.'"

"We figured you must have taken it up to the fifth floor," Derrick added.

"Lucky you didn't try to follow me in the elevator," George said. "We'd *all* be locked up in Roulain's house if you had."

"We *did* try," Derrick admitted. "But the elevator was gone. It's the kind where you need a key to call for it. We couldn't get it to come back down."

"So then how did you ever figure out what building we were in?" Shannon asked.

"Easy," Renee said, beaming. "Derrick came up with a totally brilliant idea."

George saw a tiny smile creep onto Derrick's face. A sort of proud smile.

"You?" George teased his friend.

"It can happen," Derrick said.

"Well, what *was* it?" Shannon asked impatiently.

"I told Renee to go up aboveground while I stayed by the elevator," Derrick explained. "We used the walkie-talkies to figure out which building the elevator was in."

"How?" Shannon looked confused.

"The closer Renee got to the elevator, the stronger the walkie-talkie signal got," Derrick explained.

"Ah. Roger on that," Shannon joked.

"When I figured out which building it was, I called Derrick to come up to the street," Renee added. "And then we hatched the fire-escape-and-rappelling plan of rescue!"

George chuckled. "You guys really are brilliant! Derrick, I knew there was more to you than your photographic memory."

Derrick nodded with mock seriousness. "I'm a man of many talents."

For a minute none of them moved—they just rested and tried to let it all sink in. Finally George said it.

"It looks pretty dark."

"Yeah," Shannon agreed, glancing at her watch. "It's already six!"

Everybody groaned.

Renee stood up and bit her lip. "It's so late, I think I'll have to head home before we even have a chance to look at the map."

"Me too," Shannon echoed reluctantly.

"Me three," Derrick added.

George let out a big sigh and got to his feet. "Me four," he said. "I guess that means no looking at the map tonight for any of us. We've made a lot of progress, guys, but we're only halfway there. We still need two maps."

Shannon shuddered. "This is getting a lot more serious, George."

George looked at his friend. "I know," he admitted. "But we're pyrates—remember? We'll find that treasure."

Derrick nodded gleefully. "We'll find that huge diamond. And then we'll be *rich*!"

Renee started to laugh. "All right, my fellow pyrates—so when will we get together again?"

"I don't know," said George. "We have a lot to

talk about. For one thing, what to do about Roulain. I mean, Leroy." He frowned. "Leroy might have one of the maps. He's definitely digging for something. And we still haven't talked about the rock Paul gave him."

"Oh, no—Paul." Shannon made a pained face, like she'd just bitten into a lemon. "He must be pretty mad about the Oreos."

"I'm sure he'll understand," Renee reassured her.

Shannon sighed. "I hope so."

"Well," said Derrick, "it looks like we just found a whole bunch of questions."

George nodded. "We'll find the answers, guys." He started walking toward home, and soon his friends fell into step behind him. "Hey," George said suddenly, "Derrick, I think I have a password for you to try on that handheld computer."

Derrick looked up and met his eyes. "What?"

"Roulain."

The crew's adventures continue in Pyrates №3:
<u>*Dead Man's Chest*</u>
where George and Paul explore a creepy
underground lake. . . .

"Hey, what's that?"

Paul pointed with his left hand. George followed the line of Paul's finger and saw something dark in front of them and off to the left. It looked like it might be solid ground. *But isn't that in the wrong direction?* he thought.

"Is that the other side?" Paul said. There was a note of excitement in his voice.

"I don't know." George pulled out the section of the map with the lake on it. As much as he wanted to believe they were all the way across the lake, he really didn't think they'd gone that far. Had they been going the wrong way all this time?

George knew he needed to make a decision, and fast, too. If that wasn't the shore up ahead, then they would be wasting precious time by paddling over to it. But if it was, and they went the other way, they could be out here for a very long time.

"I think we should check it out," George said finally. He hoped he sounded more decisive than he felt.

He paddled on the right side of the raft only, turning it to the left, in the direction of the shadow ahead. It took a while to get there, but it was definitely starting to look like land. George felt a rush of relief. He couldn't wait to get off this lake!

"I don't think it's the other side," Paul said with disappointment in his voice.

George stopped paddling and looked up.

"It's . . . it's an island," George said, amazed. Who would have thought there would be an underground lake under New York City, let alone one big enough to have an island in it?

A little part of George wanted to land on the island and check it out. But his common sense talked him out of it. He was already majorly late, and stopping here would just make him later.

George turned the boat back around and set off back in the opposite direction. But he couldn't stop himself from taking one look back at the mysterious island. As the raft moved slowly away, he thought he could see something on the surface of the island. He turned his bright toward it, and it slowly came into focus.

It was a tombstone.

A feeling like ice ran down George's back.

He started paddling faster.